HORRORS

I.

Companion volume to

Horrors and Hauntings in Cornwall

First published 1989
Tabb House, 7 Church Street, Padstow, Cornwall

ISBN 0 907018 60 2

Typeset by Exe Valley Dataset Ltd, Exeter, Devon
Printed in Great Britain by
The Guernsey Press Co. Ltd, Guernsey, Channel Islands

HORRORS AND HAUNTINGS
IN DEVON

An Anthology of Short Stories

Edited by

William Garnett

TABB HOUSE

Table of Contents

A Castle on Dartmoor

Walter Walkham

IN the good old days when Tavistock had two railway stations, and the trains were pulled by steam engines, Arthur and Michael travelled there from prep school for the half-term holiday. Arthur lived on Moorgate Farm on the edge of Dartmoor, not far from Tavistock. Michael was invited to Moorgate because he was Arthur's best friend, and his own parents were abroad.

The Devonshire countryside was new to Michael, with the cows trooping in for the evening milking, and each farmhouse with its own orchard. In some of the nearer orchards, he could see from the train a few out-of-reach yellow apples still on the tree-tops. The evening sun bathed the scene in a golden glow, and Michael thought how lucky Arthur was, to live on a peaceful, homely farm like one of those alongside the railway track.

At the station Michael met Arthur's father. Mr Honeywill looked splendid in his market clothes and polished leather gaiters. The boys climbed with their suitcases into a market cart waiting for them in the station yard, with Champion, a patient pony, between the shafts. Soon they were clip-clop, clippety-clopping along the road in the gathering dark, and Arthur held the reins while his father lit the brass-bound oil lamps.

Presently they turned into an open gateway, and drove along an avenue lined with beech-trees. As his father turned the cart again in front of the house, Arthur said, "Why not drive straight round to the back, Dad, and save time?"

"Your mother, my boy," explained Mr Honeywill, "likes to meet her guests at the front door."

Mrs Honeywill welcomed Michael and led him upstairs to the guest room, holding on high an oil lamp to light the way. In those days Moorgate Farm had no electricity; the power did not come until a few weeks after Michael's visit.

At supper in the warm, oil-lit kitchen, Michael met Silvie, Arthur's sister. Two years younger than Arthur and Michael,

Silvie was shy, but being well brought-up, she did her best to make conversation.

"It's Hallowe'en in three days' time," she announced.

"I suppose you'll go to the party in the village hall," said her mother.

"Oh, I don't know," said Silvie. "It's really for the younger children."

She didn't want her brother's friend to think she was too young for his company; at ten years of age, she reckoned she could mix quite freely with twelve-year-olds, provided they weren't stuck-up.

"So, said her father, "I needn't make you a turnip lantern this year."

"O-o-oh," Silvie thought aloud, "I shouldn't like not to have a Hallowe'en lantern. It's only once a year, isn't it? . . . What I should really like is to go to Castle Rock, if someone will go with me . . . Can I, Mummy?"

"We'll see," said her mother.

Michael, who also wanted to make conversation for politeness' sake, asked "What goes on at Castle Rock?"

"It's the pixies' meeting-place," replied Silvie. "Only at night, of course. You don't see them very often. Usually only Hallowe'en and May Day."

"Pixies?" said Michael. "Do you mean those fairy-like things?"

"I don't know much about fairies," admitted Silvie. "I've never seen one, that I can remember. Only in pictures. They have wings, and they make little flutters through the air. Pixies don't: they have no wings, you see."

Her brother wondered how he could change the subject. What Silvie didn't understand was that prep school boys, even if they believed in fairies, pixies, hobgoblins and the like, jolly well wouldn't admit it.

"These pixies," asked Michael; "what do they do, if they can't flit through the air?"

"They hold courts and feasts, and play music and dance in a circle. They also get up to all sorts of mischief, especially if you offend them."

Michael looked around the table. Everyone seemed to be busy eating.

"How big are they?" he asked.

Silvie put down her knife and fork, and held one outstretched hand above the other.

"About that tall," she said.

"H'm," said Michael, "About nine inches."

He looked around the table again. Arthur looked away from him. Mrs Honeywill didn't look at him, but he did catch Mr Honeywill's eye for a moment, and see the corners of his mouth turn upwards in a smile.

"You're having me on, aren't you?" he asked Silvie.

"What does 'having you on' mean?"

"About the fairies."

"Not fairies. Pixies."

"Well, pixies, then. It's all a joke, isn't it?"

"Nobody pokes fun at the pixies!" protested Silvie. "That's asking for trouble."

"Quite right, Silvie," said Mr Honeywill. "They should be treated with proper respect."

"Dad," asked Arthur, "when was the last time you actually saw the pixies?"

His mother decided it was time to intervene.

"Ahem!" she said. "Michael, could you eat some more lamb? And another potato?"

Nobody mentioned pixies again until next morning.

MICHAEL awoke to the clatter of milk churns in the farmyard.

"Gosh!" he thought. "They'll think I'm lazy, lying in bed while they're working."

From the guest-room windows all he could see was the front lawn with a monkey-puzzle tree, the beech-lined drive and the hedges beyond. Michael washed, dressed and hurried downstairs.

At the foot of the stairs he could hear Mr Honeywill's voice through the open kitchen door saying "The stable was wide open, and Champion gone. We picked up his footprints and followed them to the wood. There we found him, covered in mud, and his mane and tail all knotted."

"That's pixie work all right," declared Mrs Honeywill. "Oh, hallo, Michael! Did you sleep well?"

"Good morning, Michael," said Mr Honeywill. "You must excuse me. I'm all behind this morning."

He stamped out to the yard, obviously in a bad temper.

At breakfast, Arthur and Silvie were quiet. Michael worried that he might have offended Silvie's pixies the previous evening. Had he? All he had said was ... what had he said? Something about the pixies being a joke. It was no joke if they had really turned the pony loose and rolled him in the mud. But if they were only nine inches high, how could they open the stable door? It was all very mysterious.

After breakfast, the three young people put on wellingtons and went to the stable. Arthur worked on Champion's mane, unravelling knots, while Silvie disentangled his tail and combed it.

"Have you got a brush," asked Michael, "so I can get this mud off?"

"I should let it dry first," suggested Arthur. "Then it will come off easily."

"Do you suppose the fair ... pixies really did this to Champion?" asked Michael.

"It's just the sort of thing they do," said Arthur.

"Especially if someone offends them," added Silvie.

"Crumbs! Is there anything I can do to please them, and make up for it?"

"They do like a saucer of cream," said Silvie. "It's one thing they can't get for themselves."

"Do you think Mrs Honeywill would let me have a saucer of cream for them?"

"I'll ask Mummy," offered Silvie. "We could leave it at Castle Rock on Hallowe'en."

While the mud dried on Champion's legs and flanks, Arthur and Silvie took Michael for a walk on to the moor, beyond the highest fields on Moorgate Farm. They followed up the course of a stream which tumbled down the moor towards them and went on to water some of Moorgate's fields.

"That's called Larkworthy Brook," said Arthur.

They came to a large rock standing out of the moor, about a mile from the house. Between it and Larkworthy Brook the red-brown bracken gave way to a fine level stretch of green turf.

"That's Castle Rock," said Arthur, pointing at it.

"It doesn't look much like a castle," said Michael.

"Not by day," agreed Silvie, "but it does by moonlight. Look: do you see this ring here like a big circle on the grass?"

Michael studied the turf where Silvie pointed, and his eye followed a narrow track making a complete circle, several yards across.

"Yes," he replied. "What is it?"

"It's a pixie ring. This is where they dance."

"Have you seen them?"

"Yes. Last May Day. My Brownie friend Jill and I came here in the evening and we saw them gathering. We forgot all about the time, and it was dark when we left. Then we lost our way, and when we did get home at last, everyone had been looking for us for ages. Mummy and Daddy were very cross."

"What did they look like – the pixies, I mean?"

"They were dressed all in green, with green hoods. The girl pixies had skirts, and the boys knee-breeches."

"Did you hear them talking?"

"Yes. They talk jabber-jabber, very fast, like a cross between grasshopper noise and a lot of turkeys saying 'hobble-gobble.' You can't understand them; they all talk together at once, and only listen when the king speaks."

"They have a king?"

"Yes. And a queen. And a herald with a trumpet. They stood over there, with their backs to the castle, and the ordinary pixies stood all around."

"How many of them?"

"More than you could count; hundreds of them."

"And you think they'll come again at Hallowe'en?"

"I hope so," said Silvie. "Don't you?"

Arthur said "I wouldn't rely on it. First it has to be a moonshiny night. Then you have to be careful not to disturb them, or let them see you . . . Perhaps," he added thoughtfully, "if we did something to attract them here . . . I know! Let's build them a castle, here in front of the rock."

"It's only two days to Hallowe'en," said Michael doubtfully.

"I don't mean a castle with rooms in it," explained Arthur. "We could build it like a fort: walls on four sides like a courtyard, with an entrance arched over the top, for them to come in and out. If we made the entrance a foot high, do you think the tallest pixies would be able to walk through?"

Michael and Arthur looked at Silvie.

"Ye-es," she said, "but I don't know if they really want a castle here. What they would like is a bridge over the brook. The pixies coming from the other side have trouble crossing over. On May Day they went a long way up there to find a place where they could hop from stone to stone and keep their feet dry."

"We could build both," said Michael. "A bridge and a castle: isn't that a good idea?"

"I know where we could get squared stones," said Arthur. "From the old shippen the builders altered when they made the new milking parlour out of it."

"What about cement and sand for the mortar?" asked Michael.

"There's some left over from the new building. Mind you, I don't know if Father will let us take it. Cement is quite expensive, you know."

"I'll ask Mummy first," promised Silvie. "She'll get Daddy to agree."

"What about getting all the stone and things up here?" asked Michael.

"That's easy," said Arthur. "We'll take the tip-cart, and Champion. Come on, we'd better go back and get organised. We haven't got much time before Hallowe'en."

"THE cement, too!" protested Mr Honeywill, when Arthur told him of their plans.

"Just a couple of bags, Dad," pleaded Arthur.

Mrs Honeywill backed up her son. "You might just as well let them have it. The last time you saved some spare cement, it went as hard as a brick, and you had to throw it out."

"Oh, all right," conceded Mr Honeywill, "if it keeps them out of mischief. What else do they want?"

"We shall need Champion and the tip-cart, please, Dad," said Arthur.

"Mind you look after him properly," said Mr Honeywill, "and don't let him wander on the moor."

Silvie promised "I'll bring him straight back, Daddy, when he's finished taking up all the stones and things."

Michael could only watch in admiration as Arthur and Silvie harnessed the pony to the tip-cart. This was something he didn't know how to do, but they did, and one of them was a girl two years younger than himself. Silvie also helped to load the building materials in the cart, keeping the weight evenly balanced over the axle. In went the squared stones: long ones, short ones, thin ones, thick ones; also sacks of sand, two bags of cement, mortar mixing board, shovel, trowel, string, wooden pegs and a spirit level – three cart-loads altogether.

While Silvie took Champion and the cart back to Moorgate for the last time, Michael and Arthur started work. First they put wooden pegs at the four corners of the castle site, moving them little by little until the diagonals were the same length when measured by the string; then they knew that the corners would be at right angles.

Michael started laying out the bottom layer of stones.

"What are you doing?" demanded Arthur.

"Laying the foundations," said Michael.

"What, on top of the ground? You can't do that. We have to strip off the turf first, and any soft ground underneath. Then we can lay our foundation."

Michael soon realised that there was more to building a castle – even a pixie-sized castle – than he had thought. He and Arthur were still engaged on the wall trenches when Silvie returned.

"The bridge over the brook is more important," she said.

"In that case," said Arthur, "you pick out all the wedge-shaped stones, and put them in a separate heap. Keep the smallest ones for the castle entrance arch, and the rest for the bridge."

When dusk fell, they had only the foundations built for castle and bridge. Michael and Silvie were gloomy about the amount of building work remaining.

Arthur said "Never mind. We've done jolly well today. We've got all our materials here, and the foundations laid already. We'd better go home now. I don't know about you, but I'm hungry."

Arthur was the master builder. Over the next two days he fitted the stones together and jointed them in even courses, using the bigger stones in the bottom course and in the corners, which he called 'quoins'. Michael mixed the mortar, using three shovels of sand to one of cement, and just enough water so that it stuck to the stones like butter on bread. Silvie fetched and carried, and fretted that they were not getting on with her bridge.

By lunch-time on Hallowe'en the castle was finished, with the ramparts about two feet above the ground, corner turrets a few inches higher, and a look-out tower higher still over the arched entrance facing the brook. They had formed the arch over a wide cocoa-tin propped up on its side, knocking out the tin, after the mortar had set hard. On one inside corner of the courtyard they had built a staircase.

Silvie examined the stairs and said "The steps will be about knee-high for a pixie, but I expect they'll manage . . . When are we going to do the bridge?"

"After lunch," said Arthur. "First we have to make something to hold the bridge arch while the mortar's wet."

At lunch Mr Honeywill said, "You're very thoughtful, Arthur. What's on your mind?"

"Dad, how can we make a support for a stone arch over Larkworthy Brook?"

"How big a span?"

"Two feet six inches, Dad, and six inches wide."

"Six inches wide? Six inches? What good is that?"

"It's for the pixies, Dad . . . Silvie wants it."

"Oh, I see . . . Well, I'll help you after lunch."

Mr Honeywill found some flat pieces of iron, bent into an arc shape, from the iron tyres of an old wagon wheel, and also some wooden pieces of wheel rim with the spokes still on them.

"There you are," he said. "You can prop that up as centering for your arch. Take a saw with you, and a hammer and some nails."

Arthur and Michael carried the heavy centering up to Castle Rock.

All the way Silvie went ahead, calling over her shoulder, "Come on. Hurry up!" She only carried a saucer of cream for the pixies.

It took the boys longer than they expected to erect the centering and steady it. Then Michael mixed mortar as before, and Arthur laid and jointed the stones. They had just enough stone and sand and cement to complete the work – and just enough daylight. Dusk had arrived when they finished the bridge approaches on each side of the brook.

Arthur said, "We can leave the centering up until tomorrow."

Silvie argued "You can't leave that iron under the bridge. Pixies are terrified of iron."

After they removed the centering, the arch held, and the bridge looked like a real Dartmoor one. Silvie was delighted, and put her head down to pixies' eye level to see the darkening horizon through the arch.

They collected all the tools and the iron parts of the centering; leaving the saucer of cream in the courtyard, they departed for home. The first star already shone in the evening sky.

LATER that evening, Mr Honeywill produced a scooped-out turnip lamp for Silvie; it had a grinning face lit by an inside candle, and a loop of binder twine to carry it by. Arthur was glad his father had not made turnip lamps for Michael and himself, in case his friend thought they were babyish.

"Mind you're back by ten o'clock," said Mrs Honeywill sternly, wagging her finger at the young people.

"That's very early, Mother," protested Arthur.

"It will still be long after Silvie's bed-time," said Mrs Honeywill.

"Suppose they don't start to gather until nearly midnight," said Silvie. "We shan't see them at all."

"We can't have you out on the moor at all hours," insisted Mrs Honeywill. "It's easy to lose your way."

"It's a lovely, moonshiny night," said Arthur. "You can see for miles."

Mr Honeywill settled the argument.

"Arthur, is your watch working?"

"Yes, Dad."

"Right. Make sure you're back before midnight. That means you leave wherever you are well beforehand, in plenty of time. Do you understand?"

"Yes, Dad. Thank you, Dad."

Mrs Honeywill looked disapproving, but she didn't say anything more.

Dressed in coats and scarves and wellingtons, the young people set out in the crisp, clear evening, the moon so bright that Silvie's lamp hardly shone at all. They climbed up 'Bove Town field which overlooked the house and buildings, and the field called The Crease, past the sheep pound and on to the open moor. The moor seemed different at night, and mysterious, as though it held secrets, and challenged everyone to discover them.

Presently Arthur murmured "We'd better not talk beyond here. When I put my hand up, we'll stop and put Silvie's lamp out."

He led the way carefully. When they could see Castle Rock ahead, Arthur held up his hand, and they waited for Silvie to blow out her lamp.

In a hoarse whisper, Michael said "I can't see any pixies."

"Ssshh!" whispered Arthur and Silvie together.

On tiptoe Arthur led the way nearer to the rock, and the castle they had worked so hard to build. Soon he held up his hand again, and they stopped. He pointed across the brook. Silvie glanced at him and nodded.

Michael stared hard and long across the brook, then whispered loudly "I can't see anything."

"Ssshh!" said brother and sister again. They each gripped one of Michael's arms, and Arthur pointed.

This time when Michael looked, he could see something moving; in fact, there was more than one thing moving. The young people dropped on to their knees, and moved forward on all fours, until they were close enough to see their pixie castle and bridge quite plainly in the moonlight, and smell the fresh cement mortar. Arthur and Silvie watched, fascinated, but Michael could no longer see any movement on the other side of the brook.

'That's funny,' thought Michael. 'Just now, when Arthur and Silvie grabbed me by the arms and pointed, I could see what they saw. Perhaps . . . if I touch them again . . .'

Brother and sister being one on each side of him, he reached out and held them both by the arm. When he looked across the brook, he could see little moonlit creatures walking upright like people. They were pointing at the bridge, and they seemed to be arguing. He could hear a faint twittering noise. Perhaps this was what Silvie had meant by 'jabber-jabber' talk. When Michael let go his friends' arms, the little creatures faded from sight; he grabbed Arthur and Silvie again, so hard that they turned and looked at him.

"I can see them now!" he whispered.

"Ssshh!" they answered, very quietly.

All three watched while several pixies arrived on the far side of the brook, discussed the bridge excitedly among themselves and then moved away, going higher up the brook. None of the creatures crossed the bridge; only one ventured on to it, but he quickly scampered off again as though his feet were on fire.

Presently, the friends saw on their side a little figure come around Castle Rock and approach the new castle. Being nearer than the other pixies, his green tunic and knee-breeches clearly showed some mudstains. Cautiously he tip-toed to the entrance and peeped into the courtyard. When he glanced up at the arch, he shied away, almost as far as the bridge. Then he waved to the others across the brook, and the twittering noise increased.

More little people came from beyond Castle Rock, and gathered between the castle and the brook. Many were lady pixies in skirts and bodices, who clung together and kept their distance from the new building. A group of the little men, however, walked boldly together right round the castle. Not one of them entered the courtyard. After a while, all the little people had gone away, further up Larkworthy Brook, and no new ones had arrived.

Silvie whispered "They must be meeting somewhere else tonight. Let's walk up the brookside and find out. I'll leave my lamp here inside the castle."

ARTHUR led the way again, deeper into the moor, where Michael had never been. Presently Arthur and Silvie stopped, and he pointed towards a hill. They moved on in that direction, carefully picking their way between bracken clumps and boulders. Michael followed until they dropped onto hands and knees, and motioned him to do the same.

Brother and sister seemed to be absorbed in something happening on an open stretch of turf in front of them, with another rock beyond, not so large as Castle Rock. Michael could see nothing but the moonlit turf and beyond it the rock in shadow; then he remembered that he could see more when he touched Arthur and Silvie. He snuggled up between them and sat, linking arms.

Almost at once, Michael saw movement on the turf and heard strange music above the same twittering sound he had heard before at the castle. Now and again he heard a tiny, clear note in a confusion of noise, like an orchestra tuning up before the conductor calls it to order with his baton.

Gradually Michael's eye became accustomed to the movements on the turf, and he picked out little, green-clad creatures greeting one another, bowing or curtseying with old-fashioned grace before moving off to another part of the throng. He tried to count them, but it was a hopeless task: there were far too many of them, all moving about. The clearing in the bracken swarmed with them, restless as the sea.

Presently a tiny fanfare sounded, and the other sounds of music and twittering died away. The pixies formed themselves into a tight semi-circle, leaving more than half the clearing unoccupied behind them as they gazed inwards at the rock. The herald, standing on a stone at the centre of the semi-circle with a long post-horn raised to his mouth, finished his fanfare.

'Tara, tara, tara, taraah. Ta-ra-ra-raah!'

Out of the shadow of the rock came two little creatures more splendidly dressed than the pixies. The taller one had a white shirt below his tunic, and white knee-breeches instead of green. A brocaded green cloak hung from his shoulders, and on his head a golden crown reflected the moonlight. The other figure had a white bodice and full green skirt under a green cloak; her hair sparkled like a cluster of diamonds, and so did her feet, as she stepped onto the herald's stone alongside her companion.

The herald bowed and, stepping down from the stone, withdrew respectfully from his king and queen. The king held up a golden sceptre and surveyed the crowd, which fell motionless and silent; then he spoke in a tiny, high-pitched voice.

"Squeaky squawkity, squeak, squeak, squawk," he said. "Squawkity squoo-oo-ook, squeaky squeakity squawk!"

He paused and, getting no applause from his loyal pixies, he shook his sceptre at them. Then they all clapped, making a noise like a chorus of grasshoppers or a little wave breaking on a sandy shore. The noise obediently stopped when the king raised his sceptre to continue his squeaky speech.

This time he squeaked much longer, and some of the lady pixies were yawning behind their tiny hands by the time the king concluded with a final ". . . squookery squerk-squerk, squawky squawkity squee-ee-eak!"

A loud twittering broke out, with all the more energetic pixies jumping up and down while they clapped. As the tumult died down, the herald leapt upon the king's stone and blew another fanfare, while the king and queen retired into the shadow of the rock.

The noise changed as the crowd chanted together "Jabber, jabber, jabber, jabber, jabber . . ." Then the strange music, if you could call it music, started again, when all the instruments played a different tune. This time the young people could see the musicians: fiddlers, trumpeters, trombonists, hornblowers, pipers, bell-ringers, and drummers. The herald turned towards them and started conducting them; at least he brought the drummers together.

'Thumpity, thumpity, thump . . . thump . . . thump . . .' went the drums, and the revellers joined hands, spreading out into a wide circle, five deep, and dancing around the moonlit clearing. How long they danced the watchers could not afterwards say. It seemed a long time before the musical thumping became softer, and the chain of dancers was broken.

The musicians led the throng deeper into the moor, and as the end of the procession disappeared into the bracken beyond the clearing, Silvie said softly, "Let's follow them, and see where they go."

"Oh!" said Arthur, "I don't think we ought to be pixie-led any further."

"Oh, come on!" said Silvie. "They can't mean us any harm."

ARTHUR turned the face of his wristwatch towards the moon, and peered at it.

"Have we got plenty of time?" asked Michael.

"I can't see exactly," said Arthur.

"Hurry up," said Silvie, "or we'll lose them."

She got up and crossed the clearing to catch up the procession. Arthur and Michael hesitated for a moment, then followed. Silvie walked quite fast, leading the party even further away from the Castle Rock.

"Stop a minute," said Arthur. "Listen!"

Michael could hear nothing.

Silvie said "I can hear the music."

They changed direction and walked briskly downhill until Arthur stopped them again.

"Listen . . . Yes, it's louder now. Dead ahead."

They walked on, Silvie trotting to keep up.

Arthur, who was leading, stumbled and called out, "O-oh! Bog! My feet are stuck!"

Michael and Silvie stopped. Michael tested the ground in front of him with his foot; it was soft.

"Can you turn around?" he asked his friend.

"I shall leave my wellies behind, if I do," replied Arthur. "Can you and Silvie pull up lots of bracken, and put it down behind me?"

The two of them tore up several armfuls each, and threw them down behind Arthur. Michael walked carefully on to the raft of bracken and grabbed his friend from behind. As he pulled, he felt his own feet sink into the ground.

"It's working!" said Arthur. "I've got one foot out!"

Michael stopped pulling, to free his own feet.

"Keep pulling!" said Arthur.

"I will, when I get my own feet free," promised Michael, "I'm sinking, bracken and all!"

"Silvie," shouted Arthur, "get some more bracken! As much as you can. Keep throwing it here until we get out. Please, Silvie!"

Michael pulled his feet free and trod a mat of fresh bracken under them, as Silvie kept throwing more on to the edge of the bog.

Arthur called out, "I'm in up to my knees!"

Michael said, "It's getting firmer under my feet. I'll be able to help you soon."

Silvie fetched more and more bracken; Michael trampled it down.

Presently Arthur gasped, "O-oh! It's over my wellies. And it's co-old!"

"Hang on," said Michael.

"I wish I'd got something to hang on to," said Arthur in a trembling voice.

"Now let's have another go," said Michael, grasping his friend again, and pulling upwards and back towards the good ground.

This time Michael's feet sank only a little, and Arthur's feet started to come out, slowly at first and then so suddenly that the friends fell backwards together on to the trampled, muddy moor. Puffing hard, they crawled on hands and knees on to the good ground, and only then did Silvie stop gathering bracken.

"Are you all right?" she asked.

Michael stood up and answered, "Yes, thank you, Silvie. Only a bit muddy."

Arthur lay on the ground, gasping. Presently he said, "Thank you, Michael. And you, Silvie. I thought I was stuck there forever."

"But you're all right now, aren't you?" asked Silvie.

"Yes, thanks ... It's a pity about my wellingtons."

"What about them?"

"They're still in the bog."

"Mummy will be cross."

"Well, I'm jolly well not going back for them!" said Arthur. He stood up, and added "We'd better be getting back."

"Do you know the way?" asked Silvie.

"When we plunged into the bog," said Arthur, "the moon was on our left. If we keep it on our right and walk thirty paces, we should be well away from the bog."

They walked away, Arthur counting.

". . . twenty-eight . . . twenty-nine . . . thirty."

"Now where?" asked Michael.

"West," said Arthur.

"Where's west?"

"Find the North Star. There's the Plough, look." Arthur pointed at the sky. "And there's the North Star. Keep that on our right side, and go straight ahead."

He led the way, as usual, but walking more carefully in stockinged feet.

"Once we get to Castle Rock," he said, "we shall be all right."

Presently the light started to fade. The friends glanced at the moon behind them, and saw a bank of cloud crossing it. Arthur hurried westward until he stumbled.

"Ow!" he yelled. "I've trodden on some gorse, or something."

They stopped while Arthur sat and took his stocking off to remove the prickly stuff. By the time he was ready to move on, it was darker still.

Michael said, "We can still see the North Star, even if we can't see the ground very well. Shall I lead the way?"

"I'll never keep up with you," said Arthur, "not without shoes."

"I'll go on hands and knees," offered Michael, "and make sure I don't lead you into gorse or spiky bracken."

"Oh!" moaned Silvie. "Mummy's going to be cross, what with us being late, and Arthur losing his wellies."

"He couldn't help it," said Michael. "Come on."

On the westward horizon Michael saw a hump which he thought might be Castle Rock. He could only keep it in view with his eyes close to the ground. He went forward on all fours, making small detours to avoid bracken, gorse and boulders. It was slow work, and it seemed a long time before the hump on the horizon looked really big.

Silvie said, "That doesn't look like Castle Rock to me."

"Rocks," explained her brother, "look different from every direction."

When the hump towered black above him against the dark sky, Michael stood up. The cloud had covered the stars now, as well as the moon, and he could not even see his hand in front of his face.

"If that's Castle Rock," said Arthur, "our castle should be on the other side."

Slowly the friends felt their way around the rock.

Silvie exclaimed, "I can smell the cement!"

Soon Michael banged his knees on something hard, and he reached down to feel the castle ramparts with his fingers.

"This is it!" he announced.

Arthur said, "Find your lantern, Silvie. I've got some matches."

The friendly glow from the lantern enabled the friends to see a few yards around them. Silvie picked up the cream saucer and examined it.

"Look," she said. "They've had all the cream!"

Arthur held his watch to the light.

"It's only twenty minutes to twelve," he said. "Come on! We can just do it!"

In the glimmer of the lantern, the young people hurried down the familiar track to the back door of the farmhouse.

When Arthur opened the door, the kitchen light nearly blinded them.

"Hallo!" exclaimed Mr Honeywill. "You cut it pretty fine for midnight, didn't you? I was just going to look for you. And what's the idea of creeping about in stockinged feet?"

"I've lost my wellies," said Arthur.

"Lost them!" cried Mrs Honeywill. "How did that happen? And just look at your clothes!"

"It was the bog," said Arthur sheepishly.

"We were pixie-led," explained Silvie.

Just then the clock in the hall whirred and struck the first Dong! of midnight.

MANY years have passed since Arthur and Silvie and Michael saw the pixies, and the railways no longer run to Tavistock. You have to go by road.

If you think this story is just a fairy tale, go and see Moorgate Farm for yourself. It is on the Princetown road from Tavistock, and the name is on a white gate on the left. Get permission at the house and take the track leading east from the farmyard, through the fields called 'Bove Town and The Crease, past the sheep pound and on to Dartmoor. The cart track peters out, so you follow up Larkworthy Brook until you come to the little stone bridge proudly crossing it, which is too narrow even for a sheep.

On the left you will see Castle Rock, and on the level sward at its foot is Pixie Castle, as sound as the day it was built. The quoin stones feel sticky, where generations of wandering sheep have paused to scratch their greasy, woolly backs.

Don't follow the brook any higher, though, or you may get caught in the bog where Michael and Arthur and Silvie were pixie-led all those years ago.

Blue Unction

Walter Walkham

ON the Tuesday after the schools had broken up for Christmas, the local hunt met at Maddeford Churchtown. Maddeford being six miles away, her mother drove Hannah there in the Land Rover, towing Paint in the trailer.

The square was packed, and they unloaded Paint in a side-street. Hannah had groomed her skewbald pony until his white patches gleamed like snow and the rest of him like polished mahogany.

Angela, who had owned the pony before Hannah, arrived with her new horse. Together, she and Hannah looked over the field of hunters and thoroughbreds.

Hannah confided "I do hope Paint will be able to keep up."

"Hah!" said Angela. "Don't you worry about that! Just don't let him take too strong a hold, that's all, or he'll over-run everyone, including the fox!"

"Angela," thought Hannah, "always exaggerates."

Presently Angela complained "Oh, I do hate having my photograph taken, especially when I'm not expecting it."

Hannah looked around and saw her mother, aiming her camera at them and snapping away like a tourist. Embarrassed, she prayed for the signal to move off.

AT last the company was called to order by the horn; then, clip-clopping along a narrow lane, they followed the hounds out to the open moor. Hannah kept Paint, ears pricked, in the rear.

Presently the hounds found a scent, and led the column at a canter along a sheep-track. The short-legged Paint broke into a gallop, to keep up with the big hunters, and Hannah let him overtake several of them. This, she thought, is really fun: much better than the usual trot around the lanes, or spending most of the day on the edge of a wood, waiting for a fox to escape somewhere else!

The fun turned scary when they galloped over a ridge and headed downhill. Finding herself among the leaders and gaining,

Hannah pulled at her pony, but he threw his head up without slackening speed. She had to give Paint his head again, so that he could see the boulders and clumps of bracken ahead which threatened to bring them down. With her weight well back in the saddle and her heart in her mouth, Hannah relied on her knees to hold her while her mount hurtled downhill.

The hounds crossed a tarmac road and checked, casting about for the scent; to Hannah's enormous relief, Paint pulled up among them, stamping and snorting in a state of high excitement. Only then did his rider realise that Paint had outstripped the field.

As the huntsman arrived, he declared sharply, "The best thing you can do, miss, is put him up the hill instead of down, and gallop off some of his corn!"

"I'll try," gasped Hannah. "Sorry."

Paint objected, but Hannah managed to turn him away, persuading him to re-cross the road and go uphill. Pretending to ignore the curious glances of the riders still coming down, she waited until they had all passed, before venting her temper on the pony with tongue and stick.

"You cussed brute, Paint! I'll teach you to make a fool of me. If you want to gallop, do it now!" And she fetched him another thwack across the rump.

Galloping again, but this time safely uphill, Hannah crouched over the pony's shoulders and drove him on until he gasped for breath. Then, between Paint's ears, she saw the broken granite of the tor. As she tried to pull up, the boulders were all around her. Next she saw the rocky ground coming up to meet her.

WHEN she came to her senses, Hannah heard the distant music of hounds and horn. Close at hand, she heard the whinny of her fretting pony.

She sat up, immediately feeling a sharp pain in her side, and a wave of nausea. She bent forward, her head touching her knees, and breathed deeply. Feeling better, she turned her head and saw Paint, dripping with sweat – the sweat of fear. He was trapped, held by the forelegs and the off-hind in loose boulders. He looked at her in mute appeal, ears flat and eyes staring with fright.

Looking around in desperation, Hannah saw no help in any direction. Suppressing panic, she got to her feet and discovered a stiff, sore leg as well as the pain in her side. Hobbling painfully over the rocks to the pony's off-foreleg, Hannah knelt. She managed to move a boulder pressing against Paint's fetlock, but it slipped from her gloved hands and fell back, causing the pony to squeal with pain.

Hannah's eyes filled with tears, as she thought of Paint being put down with a broken leg; she bowed her head and sobbed.

PRESENTLY as she dried her eyes and looked up, Hannah was astonished to find that she and Paint were no longer alone.

First she noticed a pair of rough leather boots, and above them legs encased in heavy cloth gaiters. Then she saw the whole man, dressed in an old-fashioned farmer's smock and wide-brimmed hat. A grizzled beard framed a kindly old face. The stranger held Paint's bridle and spoke to him.

"There! Pretty li'l pony. Sensible, too."

In answer, Paint whickered and nuzzled his admirer. For a pony trapped by three feet, his calm seemed miraculous.

"Excuse me." Hannah asked the stranger, "How long have you been here?"

"Oh, I been around here a long time," answered the old man, his blue eyes twinkling.

"Can you help me, please, to get my pony free?"

"You'll have to do it for yourself, m'dear, since I've a-lost my bodily strength. But 'tis quite easy. Just you do as I tell you. Now, take off they gloves; put'n down there with your stick . . . Start where you did before . . . No, git a proper hold ob'm. Use your back, m'dear, so well as your arms. That's better. Put'n aside . . . There, now! That's the heaviest wan. You'm winning . . ."

Hannah forgot all about her sore leg, and the pain in her side. Under the strange old man's guidance, she freed one leg after another. Together they carefully backed Paint out of the boulders, Hannah picking up his feet and putting them down on the flatter places. At last they had him standing on good turf.

"I don't know how to thank you . . ." began Hannah.

"Never you mind, m'dear," the man interrupted. "You got a graze there on the off-fore. On the crown, see? When you get home, you want to dress'n with blue unction."

"Hannah! . . . Hannah!" called a voice which she recognised as her mother's. On the road a long way below, Hannah saw the Land Rover. Much closer, Mother toiled up the hill. Hannah waved.

As she approached, Mother gasped, "What a climb!" Then she stopped, to aim her camera at Hannah, Paint and the stranger.

"You don't mind having your photograph taken?" murmured Hannah.

The old man smiled. "That's all right, m'dear."

The camera clicked and he said, "Well, I must be going on. Good-bye, m'dear."

Mother had recovered her breath. "What on earth are you doing up here? The others are right over there." She flung out an arm and pointed. "Somebody told me they saw you galloping up this hill. Then I saw Paint's white markings through the glasses . . . Look at his foot! We'll have to get the vet for that."

"We only have to put some blue unction on it," argued Hannah. "That's what this gentleman says."

"What gentleman?" demanded Mother.

Hannah glanced across the pony's withers; then all around the tor. The old stranger had disappeared from sight.

"BLUE UNCTION?" queried the vet. "That went out in my grandfather's time! No, I'll spray the wound, and let the air get to it. I'll give the animal an anti-tetanus shot as well, just in case."

After Christmas, Hannah went to the chemist in Launceston to collect her mother's photographs. As she paid for them, she asked, "By the way, Mr Salt, do you have such a thing as blue unction?"

"Blue unction," repeated the chemist, and shook his head. "For an animal, is it? I could order you some copper sulphate, if you like, but you'd have to buy a whole big drum of it, and mix a little with flour and water to make a poultice. Hardly worth it, is it? Why not use something modern? Whoever suggested blue unction?"

"An old gentleman I met on the moor ... I've got his photograph here."

Hannah opened the folder and searched through Mother's photographs of the meet, finding the one of herself holding Paint on the tor. On the other side of the pony's head, where the old stranger had stood for the photograph, Hannah saw only the granite rocks and the sky.

The Well

Robin A Harward

The party was to celebrate Peter and Fiona's return from honeymoon. I had only come to see Fiona again. She thought of me as an old friend of the family and I thought of myself as her devoted slave. I had always loved her but there was nothing but friendship from her. She had always been too beautiful and full of life for a dull old stick like me. With her I had been hesitant, clumsy and shy; but I had always been useful to have around. When we were younger, I had been the first of my peers to have a car so I was always available for transport. I had gone to the trouble of getting a large saloon so she could fill it with her friends. A small two-seater would have been more what I wanted but it would have been too proprietorial and it would have put her off. She always liked a crowd, and no crowd meant no Fiona. I loved to be in her company so I was happy to be persuaded to come to pick them all up and take them wherever she wanted to go.

Her sudden marriage to Peter came as a shock; in my blind devotion I had not seen it coming. She had 'snogged' with many in the back of my car, Peter among them. I, of course, was only the obedient chauffeur. Oh, I had writhed and fumed but I would rather be useful to her than not be there at all. However, I had to admit that the big blonde Peter suited her. They made a lovely couple; everyone said so. Suddenly Peter and Fiona were engaged and almost immediately married. I remembered the wedding that bleak, miserable day that was only lit up for me when Fiona told me the family secret of where they were going after the reception. Then she had asked me to take their suitcases to the station as they wouldn't fit into Peter's MG.

Now I stood at the edge of the crowd, waiting and ready to be of use again.

Fiona had come in and was gaily telling us all of the wonderful sea and sun of the honeymoon. She glowed as she spoke, and her fluttering movements seemed graceful and full of charm. I watched her with my usual delight. She was asked where they were going to live. Peter was a newly qualified solicitor, and had joined a firm in Exeter, so it had to be around there. I moved nearer to hear her answer. They had been looking at houses for some time now, but they had seen some while ago a lovely little Elizabethan house on the way to Crediton. It was a dream. It had a little spinney all round it, a stream and a well right in front of it.

"Oh, it's so sweet," she said. "The whole front was covered with yellow roses and a magnificent wisteria." Both Peter and she had fallen in love with it. The owner, a recent widower, had apparently been anxious to sell and had recently dropped his price. They had spotted the house when driving back from a cricket match. Peter had driven off the main road and got lost. This was greeted with gales of laughter as Peter, a most determined, methodical and competent young man, never got lost.

"Oh yes," she said, interrupting the laughter, "he had proposed that very afternoon, but," she giggled, "that was before we saw the house. The whole thing seemed so appropriate. To get engaged and see one's dream house the same day."

We all laughed, yet the gay atmosphere seemed as fragile as a bubble.

Peter interrupted to tell us that the house had obviously still been lived in, but it had had a For Sale notice up. This had encouraged them to approach it, and as they received no answer when they rang the door-bell, they had walked around and peered into the windows. Fiona had been nervous, so they had taken the details from the notice and then gone straight into Crediton to see the estate agent. It had seemed perfect, but – here Fiona interrupted, to say that when they rang the owner he had sounded eager and helpful and *such* a nice man, so they had arranged to see the house the following Saturday.

Fiona's mother confirmed how excited Fiona had been. She had described the house endlessly and had unrepentantly and unashamedly expressed an intention of appropriating pieces of family furniture to fit into the inevitable nooks and crannies. This was typical of Fiona. She assumed that the whole world was hers for the taking and that anything she wanted would be given to her. It usually was.

She gathered the whole party round her to listen to her story. She told us that when Saturday arrived Peter had come with his new car, which he had just picked up from Exeter and they had roared off together to see the house. The tempo of the story changed here and Fiona seemed to be looking for an explanation. Her manner became nervous and rather petulant. I recognised the signs; something had gone wrong.

Peter now took over the narrative. They had arrived and knocked on the door. It was opened by an old man who, on seeing Fiona, froze his welcoming smile to stare at her. He stood there doing and saying nothing, looking as though he had seen a ghost.

"It was ghastly," Fiona interspersed, smiling and spreading her hands to display herself as if to point out how incongruous such a suggestion must be. We laughed briefly, eager to hear further details. Apparently he had let them in. He hadn't spoken. Peter had explained who they were. The man merely stared, not in admiration but almost, it seemed, in horror. Fiona beamed at us over this absurdity. Anyway, to cut a long story short, he had said that the house wasn't on the market and had bustled them out. He appeared to be in an enormous hurry and wouldn't listen to them.

"He almost pushed me out," Fiona explained, her brow furrowed with wonder.

Incredulous, interested, intelligent and flippant questions were fired at her and Peter

Peter became serious and authoritative. He had got on to the estate agent, who had been very puzzled and had promised to ring back. When he did so, it was to explain that the owner had changed his mind about selling and had given no reason. The agent had seemed as distressed as they were and had promised that if any explanation cropped up he would let them know. Peter had then got in touch with his boss, who, of course, knew all the estate agents, and he promised to look into it.

"Well," he concluded, "what do you think of that?"

The conversation immediately became general. Some told stories of the impossibilities of vendors. Others reposted with stories about estate agents and then inevitably came remarks about their enormous fees. This, of course, brought everyone on to the subject of solicitors, at which Peter defended himself gracefully, and then the conversation moved on to other topics.

I was standing in the centre of the room. Fiona was nearby. I went over to commiserate about the house. She smiled at me and took my arm in her sisterly way, telling me how shattered she had been. As she talked I saw how distressed she really was. I knew she was utterly selfish and self-centred. She always had been. To have been so gloriously beautiful all her life; to have everyone wanting to please her, everyone wanting to bask in her glow, to live in a society where everything seemed possible; no wonder she was spoilt. But that was wrong; she wasn't spoilt, she was sweet and generous by nature. She was as lovely as she looked. It was just that she had never had to consider other people. They had always wanted what she had wanted. Now she looked at me, waiting for a solution to her problem. Her enormous eyes sank into my brain. I stammered that I wanted to help, but what could I do? As I shilly-shallied ineffectually, someone came up and began to talk to her. Inevitably the crowd returned and gathered around her. Some girl asked her about her trousseau. An uncle, we were told, had always promised her a mink coat on her marriage. But now she said, animal skins were rather passé. But what could one exchange for a mink coat? Debate was joined with both flippant and serious suggestion, but before I was dismissed she gave me a look, for me alone, in which those soul-destroying eyes were full of appeal. I realised that I had had my orders. I determined to find out what I could about the house.

I left the party, and no one saw me go; but then they never did! I climbed into my car and drove meditatively home.

It wasn't long before I found an excuse to go to Crediton. I visited the estate agents Peter and Fiona had named and, on asking about houses, had my particulars taken. The price range of the house I was looking for caused a perceptible ripple of interest. I pointed out that I needed to be in easy range of Crediton, and soon I had the particulars of all the relevant properties.

It was immediately obvious which one was Fiona's. So, it was still on the market. Unlike the cheaper houses it had its own colour photographs and its particulars were printed in a little booklet, not on the photostat paper one usually gets. I picked it out. The girl who had given its details to me stated that there was a query about it and she didn't know if it was still for sale. So she excused herself and went in to an inner sanctum. Almost immediately a middle-aged man came out, florid and unctious. He was effusive. "A very attractive property," he said, "but there is some query. The vendor *was* eager to sell and we have had many interested parties but only recently he has talked about taking the house off the market. However, if you would like to take the particulars with you, I will ring the vendor to see if you may view it." To ensure promptness, I said that I had some other properties to look at, and then left. As soon as I was in my car I glanced at the document. It was called Bowleigh House. It certainly was charming; pure Elizabethan. It was E-shaped with a massively stone-built porch in the centre, as an integral part of the building. Yellow roses surrounded the large leaded windows and hung in exuberant profusion. The other side was neatly espaliered with softly drooping wisteria. The whole house nestled among beech trees, an enchanting sight.

It comprised five bedrooms, a bathroom, an accessible loft and, downstairs, a hall/dining room, kitchen, scullery and pantry, a drawing room and a gun room. Altogether it seemed very pleasant and convenient. There was a yard behind with out-buildings, a spinney and a small paddock. The particulars even mentioned the well, 'a charming period feature, recently reno-vated and in working order'. I looked carefully at the picture and saw it, a small circular stone wall with a shingle-roofed pulley from which hung a chain and bucket. It must be the right house! I could visualise Fiona in a summer dress and bonnet, secateurs in hand, filling a trug basket with roses. I contemplated this vision for a while but then pulled myself out of my lotus-like reverie and drove home.

The estate agent rang me very soon to say that the house was still on the market and would I come in to see him before viewing the property. I made an appointment for the following morning and arrived half an hour early. I was immediately shown into the inner sanctum and was pressed to a cup of coffee, after which the same florid gentleman became very conspiratorial.

The owner wished to sell but he was rather fussy about whom he sold the house to. It was a personal thing. He wanted to be certain that it was bought as a home and not for speculation. Apparently other interested parties had seen it but he hadn't felt that they had the house's interests in mind. Here he smiled, requiring me to understand the eccentricities of some of his clients. I asked in what way I would be considered a suitable purchaser. Oh, he was sure that I would be. The vendor didn't want some up-country nouveau-riche who would use it merely as a holiday retreat. I was glad to be catagorised as such a sober and worthy citizen and stated that if I sold it, it would only be to some highly respectable and sensitive young couple who would care for it and make it their home. I intended this remark to be honest but to sound jocular, and the response was surprising. The agent told me that I would be required to guarantee no resale for at least ten years. This startled me as I had never heard of anything like it. Surely no vendor could so tie up a building? But the characteristics of English Common Law were such, he explained, that such an idea was quite legal, although rather exceptional. I expostulated, saying no one could stop me from selling my own property. The agent was clearly highly embarrassed. "Actually," and here he leant right over the desk, "the vendor is rather eccentric. I believed that he was really in quite a hurry to sell. I had even persuaded him to lower the price for a quick sale; and he agreed." He mopped his brow and blew his nose. "But the house has been viewed by some impossible person that he has no intention of selling to. So he is determined that that person shall never get hold of it." I was amazed at this. Peter and Fiona? Which one of them was the impossible person? How could anyone think so? Peter's description of the owner's reaction to Fiona tied in with what the estate agent had said. But how could anyone feel so about Fiona? I asked if I might view the house and discuss it with the vendor. The agent agreed to this enthusiastically, seemingly delighted to avoid any further explanations. He gave me the telephone number of Bowleigh, and told me that the owner had recently lost his wife so was perhaps not quite himself. We parted with handshakes and courtesies and I set off home.

As soon as I got there I rang Fiona. I waited for her to come to the 'phone, palpitating with a mixture of my usual excitement that her proximity caused and the depression that I had such dismal news to pass on. But I hoped that Peter's boss might have something further. Fiona came to the 'phone eventually, apologising gaily that she had been at the bottom of the garden. As soon as I mentioned that I had been to the estate agent she interrupted me to gush her gratitude: "It was so sweet of you; you are such a kind man; but actually Peter has seen his boss and, to him, the estate agent has been rather more forthcoming. He is very annoyed with his client. The house is now up for sale at a much reduced price to anyone who will make sure that I won't get it! What do you think of that? Isn't it all horrid?" She was talking so fast that I knew that tears weren't far away. Fiona never cried when she was sad, only when she was angry. It wasn't very often, but it meant that everyone would be well advised to don protective clothing. I knew the signs, so I told her that I intended to beard this ogre in his den. I would buy the house and we could deal with the difficulties later. I loved being so positive. Fiona was delighted. She told me how wonderful I was. Peter would certainly buy it from me and of course, cover all my expenses. As far as she was concerned the house was now hers. She prattled on about putting an Aga in the kitchen, but it would have to be lichen green as all her pots and pans were that colour. Much as I loved hearing her talk, I told her that I must go in order to get on with the business on her behalf.

I rang off, and began to think. If I mortgaged my house and borrowed heavily I would be able to buy Bowleigh. But I hoped that the transfer could be achieved quickly. If the vendor was able to insist on a contract against resale and such a contract could stand up in court, which I rather doubted, I would be in difficulties, but I hoped that Peter's legal expertise could save me from bankruptcy. What a fool I was! It never occurred to me to back out. I lived to do Fiona's bidding and was prepared to risk bankruptcy just to please her – not that I really expected it to come to that. The conveyance of a house is a lengthy business and I knew that I must be prepared to lose a deposit for Fiona, although I suppose that I could probably escape even that. Perhaps she might just as easily find and fall for another house. It wasn't unlikely, but she did have tenacity. When she wanted something she wasn't easily diverted to other things.

I rang the vendor to suggest that I come over to view. He was friendly and pleasant and said he would be pleased and happy to see me the following afternoon.

I got up leisurely the following day and put on my most serious tweed suit. I cooked and ate a late and very large brunch. I checked through the particulars of the house and thought of some intelligent questions to ask. Having noted them on the particulars, I set off. I wandered up the Credition road between high banks that suddenly curved away to show a view that in my opinion was unparalleled anywhere in the world: a crazy quilting of small fields bounded by thick rich hedges, like a quilted counterpane over a recumbent female body, all hillocks, dips, and hollows. I thought that Fiona would sleep like that, all curled up, forming her bedclothes into a countryside like Devon. I had never had a chance to confirm my theory; I never would, but nonetheless I believed it.

As I came over the rise and turned down to the house I saw that it was all that Fiona had said. The sun was shining straight onto it, warming the stones and making the windows sparkle and smile. It was a house that was obviously a home. It seemed to embrace itself like a happy, contented woman. I stopped at the gate and went up the drive towards the porch. The well sat in a smooth lawn and was surrounded by a pavement of worn slates. It seemed an odd place to be. Surely, when it was dug there it wasn't intended that the water carriers should use the front door? Nonetheless, although refurnished, it looked as established and as permanent as the house. As I clinked over the gravel the front door opened and there stood an elderly man in shirtsleeves covered by an unbuttoned yellow hunting waistcoat. He had a gentle face and twinkling eyes surrounded by a mass of wrinkles, which suggested that most of his life had been spent smiling. I immediately warmed to him. He held out his hand, introduced himself, and, without withdrawing his hand, drew me into the house.

From the porch we stepped into a large living hall with a magnificently carved stone fireplace that dominated the room. In it, among wrought iron fire dogs, logs gently flickered. On a low table between two comfortable armchairs, was a crisp white tablecloth and a silver salver with a tea pot and cups and saucers. And this was the ogre's den!

He asked me whether I would like to look round or have a cup of tea first. Seeing it prepared, I agreed to the tea. He sat me down, poured a cup for me and asked if I took milk and sugar. Then, when all was efficiently dealt with, he leant back in his chair and said without preamble, "If you buy this house, will you promise not to resell it?" I was startled at this blunt approach, but intimated that I hadn't seen it or made any decisions yet. He looked at me directly and said nothing, waiting for an answer. I pointed out that almost everyone bought a house as an investment and that its resale price was pertinent. Such a clause as his made the house a poor investment. He nodded in quiet agreement, but his shoulders sagged and his warmth and friendliness seemed to ebb away. It wasn't that he appeared unfriendly but just rather lost and hopeless. I couldn't help but warm to him. I instinctively liked him and felt that he was someone to whom I could talk intimately. I decided to be honest so I told him that I wasn't really in need of a house but that I wanted to buy his, if it seemed suitable, for some friends who had recently married. I hoped that, for all my youth, my suit gave me the appearance of serious, sober opulence and the capability of such generosity. I hastened to point out the merits of the couple and how much they loved the house so that they would use it as a real home. I realised my gaffe as soon as I had said it.

"So they have seen the house? Are they the young couple who came here, with the wife who is such an impossibly beautiful girl?" Although his percipience had startled me, his description of Fiona made me feel very close to him.

"Yes," I had to admit. He sighed deeply, took a long pull at his cup and put it down. He reached for an old pipe rack and carefully selected a briar pipe. Next he took an ancient tobacco jar and meticulously began to fill his pipe. All the while I sat holding my knees, tense with anticipation. I watched him strike a match, light the pipe and pull gently until it was going and his head was wreathed in smoke. He took the pipe from his mouth and cupping it in both hands, stared into the bowl. At last he looked up and smiled. It was a gentle warming smile that forgave me all my many sins.

"You see," he said, "I can't sell this house to them because it is haunted."

I stared at him. What could I say? I realised that Fiona would be thrilled. If she knew that, it would be an added bonus. Fiona was afraid of nothing, and anyone less psychic than Fiona . . . I explained this and he smiled again.

"Let me tell you the story." He paused. "I tell you this in the strictest confidence." Here he became stern. He stared into my eyes. His softness became iron. He waited for a response from me. I hesitated; what was I to say? Although I realised that he wasn't the gentle old fuddy-duddy he had first appeared, I really wasn't willing to keep such a promise. I dislike promises especially when I don't know what I am promising.

"It really is in her interest; her life may depend on it," he said very quietly. That did it. I felt that he knew me. Somehow he knew intuitively about my relationship with Fiona. I couldn't flannel or fudge anything. I nodded. I had bowed to his conditions.

"When my wife and I came down to Devon, I had just inherited some Cornish mines. There was some life in them in those days, although now they are merely worn-out tunnels and some chimney stacks. A mere liability. I have to keep them well fenced, but tourists are always getting in. They seem to have no respect for their own safety. But then, in those days, there was enough work to occupy me and to enable me, that is us, to live reasonably. Well, all this haunting began just after my wife died, a couple of years ago," he said. "We had lived an extraordinarily happy life. She too was a very beautiful person. I loved her very much. I felt my whole purpose in life was to give her pleasure. She saw this house and fell in love with it too. I couldn't afford it and it was rather far from my work in Cornwall, but we bought it and we lived happily here ever after. She wasn't ill long. She died here peacefully and happily. Her last words were to thank me for a happy life." Here he paused and relit his pipe. He huffed and puffed, pressing down his match box on the bowl. I said nothing. No condolences or conventional phrases seemed appropriate.

"Anyway," he continued, "after she had gone I was very lost and began to live rather erratically. I am afraid I began to drink too much and frequently never made it to bed. It was at this time that I was awakened one night by voices. I looked out of this window and saw a young couple sitting on the well. He had his arm around her and he was fondling her gently, smiling and talking. My first reaction was anger at the trespass. I was about to go out and send them on their way when I realised that my clothes and appearance after my prolonged drinking bout would not lend me authority. So, as I had always done, I fell back to thinking what my wife would have done. I had rebuilt that well for her. It was a very old one that we had discovered when intending to plant a tree. I had lowered myself down it on a winch. It was hair-raising but fun." Here he smiled reminiscently and fingered his pipe as his mind lingered over the incident. "Anyway," he pulled himself together, "I left the couple to it and wished them happiness and went up to my bed."

"A few nights later I heard them again. They had got to know each other very much better. They were using the well in a way that would have surprised any well builder. It amazed me, but love will find a way." He chuckled. Then he stopped and stared at me to check my response. I tried to look intelligently interested.

"The following night they appeared again," he continued. "They were both completely naked. She sat on the edge of the well, rocking back and forth, swinging her legs. She was beautiful. She got up and ran away, around the well, taunting the young man who chased after her. He was fairly dark skinned, a foreigner I should think. His skin contrasted with her almost luminous whiteness. She dipped and swung like a ballet dancer, always sliding out of his outstretched arms. I watched from my window. As she laughed and tantalised him, I began to feel like a Peeping Tom and my shame awakened my anger. This was perhaps too much. I really must do something and send them away. But the scene was so entrancing and fairylike that I was reluctant to move. Then, suddenly, a cloud came across the moon and down came a sudden, vicious shower of rain. It rushed savagely across the lawn. But the young couple ignored it! They had completely ignored a sudden deluge. They hadn't paused in their play. They hadn't even looked up. As I watched in amazement, I realised what I was seeing. Ghosts! Her hair, which should have been drenched, was tossing and flying around, trying to keep up with her movements, as soft as silk. They were ghosts! I remained at the window in a state of shock.

"I was there to see the performance end. He caught and held her. He ran his hands over her, making her capture one long caress. She tried smilingly to retreat, but then she softly yielded. He placed her on the edge of the well and leaned over her – and then they both vanished.

"I remember, I jumped. First they were there and then they weren't. I waited awhile, a very puzzled man. I had had nothing to do with the supernatural. In fact I believe that I totally disbelieved it. My wife was fond of good ghost stories, but I never bothered with them. I only read biographies or history. I feel there is enough in life without adding fiction." He looked up at me mischievously as though he enjoyed making provocative remarks. But I found that I wasn't willing to discuss the relative merits of fact and fiction. I found that, as I listened to this story, my imagination had worked with it. I visualised this intangible and yet erotic scene. I had never heard of ghosts being erotic. My thoughts must have been plain to him because suddenly he barked out a laugh. He went on: "They came again. I watched them. It was like having one's own strip joint or perhaps a blue film or whatever. I've never been to one of them. My wife wouldn't have approved." He laughed again. "But the story doesn't end there, because later on, when the lovemaking became passionate and very personal, it was no longer a visual spectacle. I felt that I shouldn't watch and so I suppose I missed some of it. You see, some time later, I looked out again and saw that the young man was alone and was leaning over the edge of the well. His whole body seemed tense. He was doing something with the chain which was hanging down the well. He was pulling it up. His whole body was rigid with effort and concentration and his face was engraved with anguish. His hand came up to the well handle and he began to wind it up. It seemed hours. One arm in the well up to the shoulder, the other awkwardly across the pulley and winding the handle. Then he moved away suddenly and quickly. He held the handle and then

released it and seemed to dive into the well. His legs waved
wildly and he seemed about to fall in; then his knees came to the
ground and, with a heave, he rose up. He pulled the girl from
the well. One hand had her hair knotted around his fingers and
the other held her upper arm. He pulled her over the stonework.
I saw the stones squeeze her breasts and score her side. She was
limp and as he released her hair her head fell back unnaturally.
Her neck must have been broken. Her limp white body lay in his
dark, gleaming arms and he, very tenderly, closed her eyes that
were staring up so trustingly. He cupped her head in the palms
of his hands and raised her face to his. He very gently kissed her.
Again they vanished."

He sat there looking at me. I glanced out of the window and
saw the well pulley against the evening sky. It was black,
reminding me of a gallows. I shuddered. He stared at me, his
eyes wide and childlike among the wrinkles. "You see why
originally I was willing, even eager to sell." His look searched
deep into me. I was surprised, but then the realisation hit me.
"The girl. Was it Fiona?" He nodded his head miserably. I stared
at him. Of course, his story hadn't given me any real description
of the girl, only the way her hair had flowed and moved with
her. I had never seen hair like Fiona's, not even in a shampoo
commercial.

The old man rose up, leant across and felt the tea-pot. "It's
cold," he said, "but I fancy something stronger. What about
you? A whisky?" I merely nodded. I thought furiously as the old
man clinked glasses. What was I to tell Fiona? She would laugh
in delight at the story. I could see her dancing and swaying as
she imitated the dance, revelling fully in its eroticism as only the
truly innocent can do. Perhaps if I talked to Peter . . .

I told the old man that I must think about what he had said.
As I drank my whisky he told me that he would stay on in this
house rather than let Fiona come here. I suggested that he
should fill in the well. He seemed to consider this, but he was
obviously reluctant. I imagined that the effort of digging it out
would have discouraged him from filling it in again. But my
mind wasn't really on this aspect of the problem. I felt that
somehow I must keep Fiona away from this house altogether. Its
immediate charm seemed to have evaporated; the embers in the

fire grinned malevolently and even the cloth on the low table looked like a shroud. I swallowed my drink and left hurriedly, promising to keep in touch.

When I got home I decided that I must talk to Peter and Fiona's parents and put the facts to them. I had never accepted the possibility of the future being known: we all had the power to change our destinies by every act we made, and prophecies, fortune tellers and oracles were all nonsense. Perhaps an intelligent shaman could know enough of his client's character and circumstances to make shrewd guesses and have the imagination to cover his failures, but I was sure that the future was never fixed or certain. The old man had made no secret of his drinking habits and to accept that he saw an alcohol-induced hallucination was only too easy. If one knew that to drink too much would produce visions of Fiona dancing naked and not the usual mundane pink elephants, then drunkenness would really be a problem! With this flippant thought in mind, I decided that when I knew that Fiona was away I would go over to her parents, and discuss the matter with them. They were pretty level headed and, I was sure, would think of a solution. I felt my promise to the old man was no longer relevant and I ignored it never giving it another thought.

Later I rang Fiona's parents to arrange to see them and Peter without Fiona. They accepted this strange idea easily and told me that she would be away for the day on Wednesday. Apparently she was going to Cornwall to see an old girl friend. Peter was coming to lunch to settle some legal matters and so it would be perfect and would I like to come to tea? I agreed.

Wednesday came and after a light lunch I set off to drive across the moor in order to place the problem in someone else's hands. I was free to enjoy the view. The moor was looking beautiful and savage. Although the sun was out, shining on the heather, there were dark, brooding storm clouds hanging ominously over to the west. Someone was getting rain. Princetown no doubt. Suddenly the blackness was riven by a shaft of lightning. I awaited the thunder. It never came, but then everything was silent. The only noise was my car engine. The road wound on, up and down ahead of me. Sheep wandered across it, their ragged coats emphasising their dishevelled tramplike appearance. They turned and watched the car with that empty yet secret look that sheep have.

As I drove, I thought of my mission. My mind picked up the picture of Fiona. I imagined her dancing. I could see her sweep and twist, bending her neck coquettishly and flirting with her long hair. I imagined her body: those broad shoulders and those full breasts moving slowly and almost languidly as she turned; her waist, so small and almost fragile, above the swelling of her womanly hips and her long athletic thighs. As I watched this picture in my mind, I relaxed to enjoy it. I slowed up and drove gently so as not to spoil my concentration.

But the rush of a car and the angry blare of a horn jerked me into the present. I snatched the wheel and swerved too far; then I over corrected and there was a lurch and a crash and the car jerked to a stop. It was leaning over at a considerable angle. I pulled myself together, feeling fairly shaken. The adrenalin left my chest hurting. I climbed unsteadily out of the car, and realised the full disaster. I had run into the ditch and the car was balanced on granite rock. Half the car was belly to the ground with the front wheels bent at a ridiculous angle. Both the rear wheels were spinning listlessly in the air. What a fool I felt! I stood there, looking at it and cursing myself angrily. There was absolutely nothing I could do.

I looked around me and of course, could see no human habitation. I knew the road well enough to know that there was a farm a few miles ahead, so I locked the car and started walking. Eventually, footsore and very angry, I found the farm and in it a telephone. I rang the nearest garage and asked them to send out a tow truck. They, of course, said it was out at the moment but that they would come as soon as they could. I then rang Fiona's parents and told them. They commiserated, saying that Fiona had rung them earlier to say that she wouldn't be back that night so if I could get to them I was welcome to spend the night. I thanked them, and began to wait for the truck. The farmer's wife was very kind and hospitable and gave me several cups of tea, telling me that it could have been worse. I am afraid I wasn't very appreciative. It was three hours before the truck came and we went back to the wreck. They expertly and quickly winched up the front and dragged my car out of its predicament. Then I travelled with them to the garage in glum silence. The proprietor hired me a vehicle and I drove off to Fiona's parents in a battered old Ford van. It smelled not only of damp dog, but other smells I avoided identifying. Soon I arrived at the house, The hall was empty and deserted, and as I entered the living-room the silence was tangible, but the room was full. The family were sitting rigidly on the settee with Peter standing behind them. They were frozen, staring at the young policeman who stood in front of them. Then they all turned to me. Fiona's mother's face was white and pinched and she stared at me without attempting to smile.

"I am afraid something terrible has happened. Fiona has had an accident, She's dead." Her voice broke the silence and with it the awful stillness. She burst into convulsive tears and her husband put his arm round her to hold her tight. Peter had turned to look at me, looking as though he had been shot. Then he seemed to shake himself, and walked round the settee to the embarrassed policeman. He thanked him, his voice subdued and grey, for his kindness and consideration and then turned away forlornly, his face fighting emotion, looking like a lost child. The policeman cleared his throat and murmured some words in a deep Devon drawl. I don't believe anyone understood or even heard. He picked up his hat and made for the door. No one seemed to notice him and the only sound was Fiona's mother's strangled sobs. So, as I was the nearest to the door, I showed him out. Besides, I badly wanted to know more. In the hall I took his elbow to stop him and he turned towards me. My mute question caused him to glance back. He then leaned closer to me and asked in a graveside whisper if I was a relative.

"No," I answered, "only a family friend."

"Oh," he answered, looking relieved; "you see, there are some things I couldn't mention in there, just then. There are some suspicious circumstances. We shall have to look into it. The accident was reported by a young Indian tourist, who is apparently unknown to the family. He was with her, you see. She fell down a mine shaft. He caught her and pulled her up. But she was already dead. It was difficult to explain in there, what with her young husband there, being present, you see. It was very difficult, see, her being all naked."

The Cow

Robin A Harward

THE description of a plain, ordinary modern bungalow enabled me to spot it at once as I turned off the Exeter road. It stood in a slight valley, surrounded by undulating fields and enclosed in a ring of concrete posts supporting a chain link fence, whose barbarism was somewhat cloaked by convolvulus. I pulled up opposite a typical ready-made iron gate topped with a sunburst of wrought iron with a name plate on it which announced the building as Sunnyview. The sign was the only part of the house that looked fairly recent. It was as I expected.

The bungalow too was just as I expected. The roof was broad and far too flat for this climate: the gutterings were working far too hard and water was pouring over the edges and puddling the flower bed that ran along the front. A few discouraged wallflowers drooped in this bed among dandelions, which were also less than exuberant. The front door was ill protected by an inadequate porch and flanked by overlarge windows in iron frames from which the garish orange paint had faded and peeled.

As I sat and looked at it I remembered how I had first heard of this house. I had been driving back from Taunton from a meeting that hadn't taken place and had stopped at the Trout Inn in Bickleigh for something to eat, as I now had time and wasn't expected home until much later.

I hadn't visited the Trout for many years and entered, looking around me nostalgically. It had been the first pub which I could have called my 'regular'. So when I entered I had all the expectation that my youth would come back to me. But the decor had changed and the landlord was a stranger. I ordered a pint and a pasty and took off my coat and sat down near the fire. There was only one other customer, a neatly dressed, clerkish man whom I mentally categorised as a civil servant. He had a nondescript greyish suit and a forlorn moustached face. The furtive summing up in his eyes as he looked me over made me feel that here was someone who possibly might like to chat. I

needed some conversation as I had sat long in my car and hadn't
talked to anyone all day.

I greeted him and made some relevant remark about the
weather to show him that I was willing to talk. He nodded and
merely grunted, dipping his moustache into his glass and taking
a long slow mouthful. Having done this, he looked back and
once more examined me. It was a long sorrowful look and one
which warned me that this man perhaps wasn't going to be so
easy to talk to.

"Do you come from round here?" he asked suddenly.

I said that I didn't but explained that I had been born in
Tiverton and had often come to this pub in the past, but that
now I lived beyond Dartmoor. I felt that I had offered enough
information for him to ask questions. But he didn't. He merely
looked at me. This persuaded me to be more forthcoming and I
explained that the war had brought my parents west, and that I
had grown up here.

This released some mechanism in him and he began to talk.
He came from 'up country' and had bought a bungalow down
here to retire to. But it hadn't worked and he was going back. I
said that I was sorry that he hadn't succeeded in settling down,
as so many people had moved to Bickleigh and had retired
happily. I went on to say that I had often thought that I would
like to retire to the Exe valley and that this area was the one that
I would favour.

"Oh the place is fine," he said. "But I couldn't live here." I
felt this as a criticism and my local loyalty rose up but I didn't
want to discourage him from talking so I intimated that it was
often difficult to begin again in a new area, but that he oughtn't
to give up, and chatted on in this vein while he looked at me
lugubriously.

He interrupted my mundane sentiments by saying curtly "My
house is haunted. I can't sleep there."

This startled and intrigued me and I immediately asked,
"Haunted by what?"

"A cow," was his surprising answer.

His expression of stoic yet suspicious melancholy restrained
my immediate desire to laugh. I merely gawped and said,
"Cow?"

"A great big cow that bellows and dies on my carpet each night. It's a Friesian I understand," was his incongruous answer.

I was stunned by this, and searched for a response while he plunged back into his glass. The landlord was washing glasses behind me and although apparently in easy earshot contrived to wash and wipe as though our conversation was no concern of his.

My companion came to my rescue and began to explain. He had bought the house, a nice little bungalow, a few miles up the road and had moved his furniture into it. He and his wife had decided to call it Sunnyview because its original name was rather weird. He had a sign made and the first thing they had done was to hang it on the gate. They had picked up a very nice carpet in a local sale on that day and he had spent the afternoon laying it in the drawing-room while his wife had got the bedroom ready. When this had been done they had had their tea in the kitchen and had decided to have an early night and then do the major unpacking in the morning.

During the night they had both been woken by a tremendous noise and had rushed into the next room to see a cow struggling and sinking into the carpet. As they watched in horror from the door it sank and finally disappeared. They had dressed and rushed out of the bungalow and driven to the nearest building, a farm, and poured out their story. He and the farmer had gone back to investigate, while the farmer's wife had ministered to the shattered wife. They had found nothing; everything was as they had left it.

The next morning they were convinced that they had both hallucinated and they spent the day getting the home ready. By unspoken mutual agreement they did nothing to the drawing room and again went to bed early. But again the episode of the cow happened, after which he had had to take his hysterical wife back to her mother; and there she still was. She wouldn't come back and he was only here now to collect his furniture, which was in a van outside, except of course the carpet. His wife didn't want to see that again!

The story intrigued me, but as I asked for more details two more customers came in noisily and began to order drinks. We waited in silence as they settled down at the next table. They were obviously regulars and talked to each other with cosy familiarity and unconscious noise that showed they were at home.

I felt annoyed, as their presence obviously inhibited my companion. But he leant forward to explain that he hadn't sold their house 'up country' and that they would move back into it. But how was he to sell this house down here? I commiserated with him, and asked if he had thought of exorcism. This puzzled him and as I explained I became aware that my neighbours had stopped talking and were plainly listening. I felt I couldn't stop but as I continued I realised I had lost my intended audience, who finished up his drink, rose hastily, nodded to me and left. I found that I was now on my own, being watched by a speculative audience. To explain, I asked if anyone knew of a bungalow nearby called Sunnyview. This produced no reaction; no one had heard of it. One of the drinkers asked me if that other chap had ghosts. They had obviously heard enough of the story to be interested. The tale was alive enough in my mind and although I realised that it oughtn't to be spread around if the little chap was to sell his house easily, I felt no loyalty to him and was still engrossed by it, so I briefly sketched in the story. It caused considerable merriment, and as we began to joke and speculate about it the door opened and my former companion looked in. He stared at me in horrified disappointment before retreating, shutting the door behind him. Again there was a short silence, until it was broken by hearty guffaws. Feeling rather ashamed, I drank up, paid my bill and left.

All the way home the story revolved in mind. The little man hadn't been spinning a yarn. His whole manner indicated that he believed all that he had told me. I had heard of hauntings by animals. Devon is full of Black Dog legends and horses figure frequently, if only as transport for headless gentlemen. But a cow, and a Friesian, as my poor friend had so pedantically pointed out, was an intriguing idea.

The locals hadn't heard of the house, but Sunnyview was the new owner's name. Hadn't he talked about the sign? He had, I remembered, said that the old name was weird. That was a strange choice of word, and it interested me. Why weird? It was apparently a fairly new bungalow.

I thought no more about it until a week or so later when I had occasion to drive east again on business. As I was fairly close to Tiverton I drove through it for reasons of sentimentality. I like to see changes of shops and road routes that always seem to happen during absences. I parked in the first space I saw in the main street and got out to look around me.

"Good heavens, where have you sprung from?" came a voice from behind me. I turned around and a wizened old face peered up at me. Its head was glistening bald and the wrinkled nut-like face rose out of what appeared to be an outsized collar. For a moment I was nonplussed, but the neck and collar brought recognition. It was old Anstruther, known as the Tortoise, my old Latin master. He hadn't changed, merely shrunk, and this surprised me. Twenty years ago he had towered over me, terrifying me. He used to wither me every time he opened his mouth and now he was bouncing around me like an excited puppy. I greeted him with, to my surprise, warmth and pleasure. I suggested, after the initial remarks, that we go somewhere and have a talk. He suggested, a 'local hostelry' in his familiar pedagogic way and bustled off down the road. Whirling back to see if I was following, he swung into reminiscences of the old days, interspersed with questions as to what I was doing now. As I had been at school further east I was puzzled at his presence; but he also had retired to Devon. He now lived alone with his books and was coaching the occasional child for Common Entrance and 'O' levels. As he talked I was disconcerted to find myself slipping back into the role of schoolboy again. But after my first pint and his schooner of dark sherry we both relaxed. Nonetheless our conversation was broken by lengthening silences. I found that a lot of names that he threw at me meant nothing and as my memories of school were not as exultant as his, our silences increased embarrassingly. I remembered that he had been accustomed to telling us ghost stories or folk tales of the area and had once written a book that we all had been encouraged to buy. Many of us did so only to be confounded by its scholastic manner and heaps of erudite footnotes. I still had it but I had never opened it again. The memory prompted me to refer to his studies and this triggered off a fresh spate of speech. He was writing another book dealing with the legends of the West Country and had that day been searching the local library for material. This was too good an opportunity to miss and I began to tell him the story of the cow. It didn't produce the expected jocularity. He listened with fascination and began to ask very pertinent questions, none of which I could answer. "Where was the building? How old was it? What sort of building? What was the owner's name? How old? Were there any other witnesses?" He was obviously more than interested. He said that he had read most of the local stories in this area. He explained that animals often featured as ghosts, but he hadn't heard of a cow before. He also explained that the Friesian was a relatively modern breed in England and therefore this seemed to be a modern ghost story. He began to talk of modern folk lore and referred to phantom hitch-hikers, ghost trains and even Second World War aeroplanes; ghosts apparently didn't have to be antique.

His whole attitude showed a genuine and even enthusiastic interest; we obviously weren't just chatting. He asked all sorts of questions and made notes of my vague answers on an old envelope. I began to realise that I must move on so I steered the conversation back to ourselves. I got his address and telephone number and gave him mine, and promised to keep in touch. I left him musing over his rough notes.

A week later he rang me up in the middle of a television play, to my annoyance, to tell me that he had traced the bungalow. It had originally been called Jenny's Bottom! Apparently the field had always been known by that name and the builder had unselfconsciously so named the bungalow. Amid my laughter he explained that bottom often referred to any low lying land and that Jenny had once been the mistress of the landowner who had paid her off with this field. And so the name had remained, which my civil servant had been so reluctant to keep. In the 1930s, apparently, the area of the bungalow had been fenced off from the main field and when the farm had been sold the new owner had built a bungalow for his then cowman; but the cowman had never lived there as he had been killed in an accident just before he was due to move in. It had then remained empty until recently when it had been put up for sale and sold to someone up north who had bought it to retire to. It was now back on the market. We both assumed that I had met the 'someone up north'. But there appeared to be no local awareness of the ghost. He was very excited by all this information and began to explain the exact position of the bungalow. He intimated tactfully that I ought to go to see it as he hadn't got a car.

My annoyance at his interrupting my play had somewhat dissipated. I still felt I didn't want to become a ghost hunter but had to admit to him that I was planning to go to Exeter the following week. I soon allowed myself to be persuaded to press on to Tiverton, collect Anstruther and then return to Bickleigh to have a look at the bungalow.

We arranged a time of meeting, on Wednesday at midday, and I then returned to my play; but I no longer understood it. As the figures on the screen continued their intense and apparently purposeful activities my mind wandered back over the tale. Could the death of the cowman be relevant? Surely it wouldn't be difficult to find out how he had died and whether a cow was involved.

I began to search my mind for knowledge of ghosts and remembered a suggestion that sufficently powerful events leave grooves in the atmosphere like the tracks on a gramophone record. Apparently, a psychic person could tune into them. I thought that if the violent death of a human being could leave such traces behind, then surely the equal agony of an animal's death could leave the same traces. But perhaps only another cow could pick them up? This amused me, and I wondered whether I ought to bring a cow with me on Wednesday.

I thought no more until Wednesday, when I quickly finished my business in Exeter and set off for Tiverton. As I came towards Bickleigh I turned up towards Silverton, on the road that Anstruther had indicated, and I quickly reached the bungalow. It was as I said, a plain, ordinary, cheap modern bungalow.

I sat and looked at it through the drizzle. It didn't look even vaguely haunted; depressed, yes, but there was no half timbering, no crenellations, no thick ivy, none of those adjuncts to the supernatural that might be thought necessary. Nevertheless I decided to go to pick up Anstruther, and get the key from the estate agents named on the For Sale sign.

I drove back onto the main road and on into Tiverton where Anstruther was waiting for me, and together we went to the estate agents, whose office was opposite the Town Hall. The rather pretty girl at the desk smiled professionally at us but seemed to have trouble finding the documents and the key. She disappeared into an inner office. Presently she returned with a young man, betweeded and exuding would-be efficiency. He told us that the bungalow had just come on the market, and he asked me the reason for my interest. This took me aback as I presumed that neither Anstruther nor I looked like possible purchasers of that sort of property. I invented a mythical housekeeper who, on retiring, wished to settle in the Exe Valley, at which he read out the details with professional briskness. Anstruther asked why it was so quickly back on the market again. This made him hesitate but he recovered well. He told us that the present owner's wife had become ill and had had to remain in Birmingham. It was unlikely that she would ever be fit enough to live in the country. It was such bad luck as they had absolutely fallen in love with the house. He explained that it would need decorating as it had been empty for some time. As he handed over the keys he pointed out that the sale included a rather fine carpet in the front room.

As we drove back to Bickleigh I told Anstruther that I had already seen the house – that I had been unable to resist the impulse to look at it while driving so close to it. He eagerly asked for my impressions. How had I felt? Did it have an aura? I was unable to give him any satisfaction. We drove on through the lovely rich Devon countryside with its little hills, little fields and little lanes and its wildness. The rain had stopped, leaving an aftermath of bright shining clarity; the sun was clear of clouds and everything seemed bright and smiling. It did not feel a time to be looking for ghosts. The rich red soil looked so self-consciously fertile, the lush green hedges so carefully tended and the grass so abundant that I almost envied the cows that swished and munched contentedly on either side of us. There were many Friesians among them but also a number of massive placid red Devon cows. Why hadn't this ghost been a red Devon? I mentioned this to Anstruther, who laughed and told me not to expect real ghosts to emulate fictional ones. He went on to tell me he had heard of an Indian haunting a house in Norfolk. This made me look at him with surprise. Did he really expect to find a ghost? Did he really believe in this cow? I now began to ask myself questions. Did I believe in ghosts? Surely not. I believed that people saw ghosts, saw fairies, even unidentified flying objects, but surely they only existed in the imagination. I remembered once when I had had to walk down a country lane in the dark, how I had followed the path by staring between the tree tops and how I had fallen into and splashed through puddles, become disorientated, and caught myself on brambles that had slashed and held me with what seemed deliberate malevolence. I had listened to the sound of the wind in the branches and had heard branches rub and creak against each other conspiratorially. Birds had cheeped, screamed and muttered to each other. Pheasants had run through the leaves like fairy cavalry. Cows had snuffled and wheezed and moved suddenly and thunderously: all these sounds could, to the medieval mind, have been hobgoblins, headless horsemen, stolen babies and all the over rich curiosities of fairy tales. I had realised that these sounds could have driven me into a panic – could have made me run blundering into unseen obstructions that would have seemed to be trying to hold or hit me. Then, if I had been able to reach my destination, I would have had irrefutable evidence of demoniac activity. No, ghosts only existed in the minds of people who wished them, unconciously or no.

I looked at Anstruther, who was watching me curiously. I explained my feelings to him. He nodded and merely answered " 'In my Father's house there are many mansions: if it were not so, I would have told you.' John 14: 2." He said this with an air of quiet finality that precluded any answer. In any case, I find that when anyone quotes the Bible at me it silences me very effectively.

We drove on in silence until we came to Bickleigh and over the bridge. I always attempt to slow down here to look at the river and I always meet an on-coming vehicle, which means I have to drive with care and concentration and am past the river before I have had a chance to see anything. Inevitably the usual thing happened, and I had to get past a tractor and trailer. This caused us to discuss road widening and the despoliation of the countryside, expressing different opinions until we reached the turning into Silverton, which we took with a change of gears and a feeling of expectation.

We came to the house; I pulled up and we paused for a moment to look at the place. I glanced across at Anstruther to see his reaction. He showed no excitement, but was looking at it with the expression he had used so effectively to quell an unruly class. The bungalow looked back impassively. We got out and went through the gate, with its cheerful sign, and walked up to the front door. It opened easily and we stepped into a long bare hall with tall narrow doors on either side. We looked into a room on the left. It was obviously intended to be the dining-room as it had a door opening off it that was open and through which I saw a sink. We went back into the hall and through the door on the right. Here was a dingy room with a fireplace of hideous creamy ceramic tiles. The whole room was lit up with a blazing red, orange and blue Persian carpet full of spirals and unending curves: the famous carpet. I stepped gingerly on to it and walked over to the main windows. These were large and obviously intended to make the most of a view. But they looked out over a small square overgrown lawn, straight at the chain link fence with a large bare field going straight up to the skyline. There were no trees or hedges, in fact nothing to look at. The sun was going down and most of the field was in shadow with that curious fluorescent greenness that evening light brings out in Devon.

"Can you feel anything?" asked Anstruther. "No," I laughed, "except what a dismal place to choose to live in."

"Why do you say that?" he asked with his eyebrows popping up interrogatively.

"I don't know. It just seems a typically unimaginative place to put a house; good enough for a cowman, I suppose."

"You must curb your radical tendencies," he smiled. "Not many employees get a bungalow built for them." I had to agree. But I asked him if he knew any more about this cowman.

"Only that he was said to be a good one. He was a local man and his death was a great shock and loss to many people round here."

"Do you know how he died?" I asked.

"Not altogether," he answered. "It was in the local papers at the time. I looked them up in the newspaper office. He apparently left the farmhouse after supper to go to check the cows, as was his wont. He intended to look in at the bungalow that was nearly finished on his way. He never came back, and was found hanging upside down from a barbed wire fence; that one over there, I suppose," he said, pointing out of another window beside the fireplace. I was looking up at a steep bank with a gnarled and bent oak tree growing at the top. The tree had a number of strands of barbed wire joined to it, evidently to prevent cattle from falling down the bank.

"He must have been trying to climb over it." I spoke musingly. I imagined how one could easily lose one's balance when climbing over wire. In this case one wouldn't fall a few feet to the gound. Here one might, if caught, fall or hang over the bank. I shuddered as I thought of the man's predicament. He had perhaps hung there all night, to die of exposure.

"Hypothermia they called it in the papers, but why on earth was he trying to climb it? There's a gate a hundred yards down the hedge." Anstruther asked this question in answer to my unspoken thoughts. I suggested that we go over there and have a look. We went out of the front door to the gate and up the road. We found a gate, climbed it and crossed a corner of a field towards the oak tree, which effectively hid the bungalow from our view. When we arrived at the wire we could see the bungalow below us, and found ourselves looking through the window straight at the surprisingly well-lit bright carpet. I realised that the light came from the other large window. From here one could see almost every detail of the drawing-room. I pointed this out to Anstruther, who merely grunted and turned back. We walked back together to the car, when I said that we ought to have brought a tape recorder and left it in the house to see if any noise was recorded. His answer surprised me.

"We have. We have all we need in the car." I then remembered his haversack. He had produced this when I met him and I had heaved it into the boot and forgotten it. I remembered wondering about it at the time, but the estate agents had put it out of my mind. We now took the haversack to the house. Anstruther went into the kitchen with it while I looked into the other rooms. They were empty. I went back to the kitchen and found Anstruther unpacking his haversack. From it he produced two rugs, two air-beds, two old lunch boxes, a bottle of whisky, a tape recorder and a flash camera. I stared in amazement.

"You intend to stay the night?"

"No," he answered with a sly twinkle. "*We* intend to spend the night." I gaped at him.

"I am sorry that we aren't too well equipped, but I thought that if I brought too much, you might have demurred."

'Demurred,' I thought; 'too right – I would have.' But he was still able to exert the authority that he always had. And I merely thought how uncomfortable I was going to be.

"I really ought to ring my wife; she is expecting me and she will worry."

"I anticipated that," he answered. "Go down to the Trout. It won't take long. Ring her from there and bring back some hot pasties. But do be quick. I rather expect the manifestation won't keep us waiting for long."

'Manifestation!' I thought, as I drove to the pub. My cow was now merely a manifestation. But the old devil had planned well. If I had known his intentions I would not have come. But here I was, saying yes sir, no sir, in no time. How was it that schoolmasters developed that effortless authority? Did they learn it or was it something they were born with? But then I remembered, with a grin, that there were many who didn't have it at all. Where had I heard that schoolmasters and lawyers were the most dangerous people in the world? It was because most revolutionaries came from amongst them. I chuckled at the idea of Anstruther manning a barricade, but was chastened to realise how easily he could send me, or others like me, to defend his barricade while he plotted and schemed well behind the lines. Although to do him justice, he was helping to man this one.

I didn't waste time at the Trout but merely looked about to see if my civil servant or any of the other ribald customers were there. They weren't, and the landlord provided two pasties, some sandwiches and crisps with no comment or recognition. I rang my wife and explained that I was held up and would be back tomorrow and rang off quickly to avoid explanation.

When I got back I was surprised to find a meagre glow coming from the windows and found that Anstruther had put candles around the dining-room and lit them. He had blown up the air-beds and arranged the rugs on them. He was squatting on the floor for all the world like an ancient witch doctor, fiddling with the tape recorder. He didn't look up but merely said "My presumption is as follows: the gentleman and his wife had an early night and were woken by the cow, while the farmer, whom they went to, was able and indeed willing to come down here to see what had happened, not having yet gone to bed. Farmers don't usually go late to bed. So the manifestation won't be too long in coming."

It seemed a reasonable conclusion. But the prospect of the early arrival of the manifestation, as I now named the cow, began to unnerve me. I remarked on the intelligent selection of supplies and divided the pasties, sandwiches and crisps that I had bought. He again apologised for the inadequacy of the preparations. I indicated the bottle of whisky and said that its inclusion would make up for any deficiencies.

"Ah ha," he laughed. "We can have one small one now, but leave the rest for afterwards." One now was a cheering thought, but the rest for afterwards was either a generous or a very pessimistic idea.

He lifted the tape recorder and showed me the button that was to be pressed as soon as we heard anything unexpected. "It should run for an hour, which ought to be enough."

'I jolly well hope so,' was my thought.

He then opened one of his lunch boxes and and produced two small glasses wrapped in tissue paper, carefully wiped them, and poured out two reasonably generous tots. There was water in the kitchen but his glasses were of the Western saloon variety; there was only room for whisky. He passed one to me, raised his in a cheerful toast and then gently sipped it. I did likewise, and felt the reassuring bite lie on my tongue and the warmth slide down my throat and spread through me. I realised that it made me feel a lot better. This now really seemed an amusing adventure but I hoped my explanations to my wife tomorrow would satisfy her. We had to have a ghost or else my story would be very lame. I could imagine her incredulity as I explained that I had sat up in an empty house with an elderly schoolmaster awaiting the death of a ghostly cow!

We shared the food and Anstruther explained that he had lit candles here so that we could have light to eat by. But when we had finished we would put them out. He didn't want our night vision spoilt. I looked at my watch; it was approaching six o'clock. The candles were making eerie shadows, and although there were five of them their light wasn't really good enough to read by. How spoilt we were by electricity! It was all too easy to believe in ghosts by candlelight. Our ancestors' fears did not seem so silly when viewed in their own circumstances.

Although it wasn't really dark outside, our candles, by contrast, made the glass of the windows stare back at us opaque and black. I got up and went to look out. The sun was well down now; the moon was coming up and the lawn and fence had that colourless silvery look that moonlight brings, a deep contrast to the warm yellow candlelight inside. I mused quietly on the simple effects that the products of modern technology, like electricity, had brought, but what immense changes they had wrought in our attitudes and outlooks.

Anstruther crunched his crisps and in the silence the noise sounded like a landslide. All our movements seemed noisy, clumsy and disturbing. There seemed no sounds of nature; the birds had gone to bed and even the obligatory owls had evidently missed their cue. Anstruther champed on. It seemed that we were the only living things anywhere.

"We can blow out the candles now," he said as he fastidiously brushed crumbs from his knees. We did so and sat down in the silence, watching the red eyes of the candle wicks blink out. Now there was nothing. Anstruther breathed a little wheezily and slurped some whisky. We sat still in the dark. As we watched, our pupils expanded and the room became curiously lighter. Everything seemed held in suspense. I realised that I was holding my breath. I didn't think that I could stand this for long. But nonetheless I felt relaxed. Anstruther had taken charge. I had no decisions to make. I would merely do or die: a silly phrase, but it sent a slight shudder around my shoulders.

At that moment all hell broke loose. There was a booming moan repeated again and again with slushy splashing noises around it. Anstruther leapt for the tape recorder and signalled me up. I sat frozen. The bellowings sounded hoarse and low, mixed with a sort of scream and a sigh. These unearthly sounds were intermingled with splashes and slaps. I was horrified, but I followed Anstruther automatically as he quickly crossed the hall and opened the drawing room door.

There was the cow in the middle of the room. It had sunk into the carpet up to its hocks. It appeared trapped. As it exerted its hind-legs, it tipped onto its face which sank into the heaving, lurching carpet. It rose up, drew up a foreleg, stretched it out and collapsed again into the carpet. There was a genuine splash as its leg struck the carpet, which rose as though liquid. Its hocks were now well down and the carpet heaved and chuckled malevolently around its quarters. There was a blinding flash of light as Anstruther's camera went off. All was dark for the instant as my eyes adjusted. Then the cow turned towards us. Its terrified expression glazed in its soft gentle eyes. Its mouth was opened wide as it bellowed its terror and it cheeks stretched to encompass the sound. It heaved again, and slipped sideways into the carpet. Its neck stretched out along the carpet and it seemed to balance for a second. Flash went the camera and in that flash, I saw through the window, a man, by the oak tree. He was climbing the wire and calling to the cow, "Steady girl, whoa my old lady." then he was gone. The cow was silent as she lay still. Her quarters were beneath the carpet, one hind-leg stuck up pathetically. Her face was half under, one eye staring at me, enormous and terrible in its appeal. Then there was a sickening slurp and the whole head went under. She heaved it up and gave a low desperate moaning cry. Steam came from her moist lips and nostrils and down she went again under the carpet. Her belly remained like an island for seconds until the carpet burbled and spat and closed over the hump. The camera flashed again and in that instant I saw the figure of a man hanging by the ankle spinning as his wildly gyrating arms gave him momentum. My eyes cleared again and the carpet was scarcely to be seen. It lay still, smooth and unrumpled. There was silence, except that my heart drummed on my rib cage as though it were fighting to get out. I was out of breath, my body was stiff and cramped as though I had run a race. Sweat was wet at my armpits and I felt as cold as ice.

"Magnificent," was Anstruther's remark. "I have never seen such a manifestation." I was shocked at this callousness. I felt I had seen a disgusting death and not only of a cow. Had Anstruther seen what his flashlight had shown at the window?

I walked back to the next room and lit the candles, all of them. I poured out a glass of whisky and drank it straight down. I poured another somewhat shakily and took the other glass and poured out a third as Anstruther came in and handed it to him. We sipped in silence.

Anstruther bent over the tape recorder, switched it off, rewound it and switched it back on. There was nothing and then the sudden rustle of movement and clatter of shoes on bare boards. Then nothing, just the tape whirring through its spools. Then came the slight screech of a bottle top, followed by the gurgle of a bottle; my restorative drink.

"But how on earth . . . ?" I expostulated. Anstruther smiled bleakly.

"I don't expect to find anything on the film either."

I was bemused. Here I was, exhausted and shocked at something that hadn't happened. We talked quietly and decided to pack up and go. It wasn't ten o'clock. As we drove back to Tiverton, I told Anstruther what I had seen through the window. This he hadn't seen as he was concentrating on the cow. He suddenly gasped and said "Do you realise what you have seen?"

"Yes," I answered, "a ghost."

"No," he said, "a ghost seeing a ghost." I was puzzled. "Look," he said, "some cow must have died here, on this spot, some years ago. It has continued to haunt this place but no one has seen it, as it is so out of the way. No doubt this part of the field was fenced off to keep other cows out of the bog. Then the new owner, seeing this waste land, decided to build on it to accommodate his cowman. It is perhaps the only non-productive piece he has. The cowman walks over to see his new bungalow, sees the ghost cow dying, now in the living room of the new bungalow, tries to rescue it and dies himself. What you saw were two ghosts of different vintages."

I stared at him. I didn't like this at all. Surely this meant that I was psychic or something. I didn't want to see such things.

Anstruther continued to talk quietly about what we had seen. He wanted a clear description of the cow's markings. I found that I wasn't sure. I could only remember the tragic appeal in those anguished eyes and the twisting body that swung from the wire. Both facts were hideous enough, even when original and one was perhaps able to help. But to watch such a thing and to be helpless, that was too awful.

I said goodnight to Anstruther; we shook hands; I ventured to wish him a good night's sleep. But my mind was taken up with devising a route home, keeping a good distance from the Moor, with its own wealth of stories of ghosts.

IT was some weeks before I was in the area again and I turned off the road and drove up to the bungalow.

The sun was shining and the whole place seemed quiet and placid. I came upon the bungalow and saw that it was dominated by a new estate agents' sign which was obliterated by a sticker triumphantly saying Sold. So the little vendor was out of his predicament. I still wonder if he had the ghosts exorcised.

The Hare

Robin A Harward

HE had first seen the hare in the field outside his farm yard. It was unusually large and had looked back at him with a curious and unexpected insolence. Hares, in his experience, were excessively timid and their wide-apart eyes usually had a vague yet manic expression. But this one had sat up and gazed at him with no fear. They had stared at each other for a significant time until the hare had turned away, almost derisively, and loped off to disappear into the young hay, towards the cottage.

It had disturbed him a little, adding to the general discomfort he felt because of the row he had had with Mrs Trevisard, which still rankled and churned inside him.

Mrs Trevisard lived in the small cottage just below his farm. It had once been tied to the farm, but he had sold it to her for what had seemed a bargain. But what a mistake that had been! She hadn't been local, and came from another part of Devon. It seemed reasonable to take every advantage of her – she had seemed unaware of it and had let him – but once the property had been sold, she had demanded her rights and had even sued him. And, to his horror, had got back more than her rights. Rights of way, here there and everywhere. Water piped over his land, electricity laid. He had even had to dig drains to take surface water away. He had been forced to agree to maintain the track to her cottage and to a standard far beyond his own requirements. Mind you, he hadn't done it. But she might yet enforce it. She was obviously very willing to go to law and seemed to have enough money to do so. The sale had been a thoroughly bad deal. Last year she had even reported him to the RSPCA for neglecting his animals! The Inspector had been most unpleasant. Interfering busybody! Anyway it had all been a bloody nuisance.

And yet she had seemed a nice enough woman to begin with. Over-educated and very sure of herself with her 'hoity-toity' voice. She called herself Mrs Trevisard although there was no sign of any Mr. She had a few guests who came in big cars and were never from around here. She bought expensive foreign food from the town and seldom used the village shop. She never ate meat and spoke contemptuously of those who did. She wore funny old-fashioned yet expensive clothes, and for all that, she was a handsome woman with a full deep laugh – a laugh that was too often directed at him.

She had many strange ways. In the summer she was said to have gardened naked; some of the local children had seen her gathering flowers at night and had sworn to it. They said she had seen them, that she had merely laughed and done nothing about it. But for all the rumours about her, most of the village people seemed to like her.

Just after her arrival, young Mrs Piper had trouble with her baby. It was born too early and she couldn't be got to the hospital, owing to the snow on the roads that year. But Mrs Trevisard had arrived and taken over. The baby was safely delivered long before the midwife got there. The doctor, who had to be got in by tractor, had said that but for Mrs Trevisard both mother and child would have died. It was said that the Williams boy, who had stopped talking after falling out of his parents' car, had been put right by Mrs Trevisard. But that was to believe a lot. Nevertheless the Williamses believed it and looked up to her.

Although everyone seemed to like her, he was certain she had it in for him. Most women gave in to him when he shouted. His wife Mavis had always been frightened of him; he had only had to hit her once and she had been a good wife since. But Mrs Trevisard obviously wasn't afraid of him. Rather, he felt oddly afraid – almost in awe of her.

Their row had been about his fence. His cows had been leaning on it to get at her flowers. She said that there wasn't enough grass in the field. That the fence wasn't stockproof, and she required him to mend it. She also added that he ought to supplement the cows' food with cake, hay or silage. If he didn't she would have to report him again. Then he had lost his temper and raged at her. She had just stood her ground and watched him with an expression of distaste. He had yelled all sorts of obscenities. She hadn't been shocked, but her distaste had increased. When his limited range of expletives had run out, he had ended flatly and somewhat anticlimactically by calling her a "bloody witch". At this she had laughed and said – he remembered the words – "Thou be better hadst thou never met with me". These strange words she said very carefully and with an intense look, that contrasted with the laugh. It had jolted and unnerved him and so he had retreated.

Since then, although he had done some vague repairs to the fence, he had avoided her.

It was the hare that evening that had reawoken his uncertainty and resentment. It had somehow brought back the unease. Although why it had reminded him of Mrs Trevisard he had no idea.

He had eaten his dinner morosely and sworn at his wife when she wanted to watch a popular television programme. He didn't care much what he watched but he needed to bully someone and his wife was the nearest and easiest. The evening passed in silence with him sunk in his chair, smoking furiously, and his wife nervously watching an almost silent television set.

The following evening when the telephone rang he ignored it. His wife went to answer it and came back to say it was Mrs Trevisard. "The cows are in her garden. You must come and get them, or she won't answer for the consequences." He rose in fury from his chair and went to put on his boots. He was rigid with anger, and grabbing his stick he went out into the yard and through the field. Most of the cows seemed to be in it but as he came over the top he saw Mrs Trevisard, standing in the hedge with a walking stick held across her body. She was wearing a long flared dark green dirndl skirt, a loose white blouse girdled with what seemed to be yards of red cord, and black pointed boots. Her hair hung loose and full, straight down over her shoulders and over her full, deep bosom. This was rising and falling with righteous anger. Her eyes were sparkling bright and caught the sinking sun, flashing with the same brilliance as her necklace, a silver crescent moon around her neck. She looked magnificent, and the farmer's anger was quickly dissipated. He stood still, awed by her. Her stick was an antique gentleman's cane and this she pointed at him saying, "Look at this mess!" He looked. Her garden was trampled, her roses knocked over and her laburnam tree lying on its side, its trunk snapped in the

middle. Its racemes were broken and scattered. A small rhodo-
dendron bush was totally destroyed.

"If those cows break in again you will live to regret it. Now
get this fence mended properly. None of your corrugated iron or
bedsteads. I want it done decently and efficiently." With this, she
turned away and marched off with the bearing of a queen,
towards her cottage. His eyes followed her; she was indeed
magnificent. Her square shoulders were masked by that mane of
heavy, tawny hair. Her waist was surprisingly slender above
heavy buttocks that moved as though they were not encased in
much beneath the skirt. She was indeed a handsome woman. Her
anger had given her a real majesty.

He pushed back the broken branches and tied them with some
binder twine. His anger was strangely muted: he seemed
spellbound. He cut and laid some of the tall hazel wands but he
knew that he would need some poles to set in it to make it firm.

'To hell with it,' he thought, having surreptitiously looked back
to see if she was looking: she didn't appear to be. He stumped
off home to take out his mortification and his foul temper on his
wife.

As he approached his yard his dog ran to meet him and
welcome him. He swore at it, and as it danced about him he
kicked it. It gave a yelp and ran into the barn. He threw his stick
into his muddy porch and stamped straight into the living room.

He went to a cupboard, took a bottle of whisky and poured
out a tumbler. He threw himself into his chair and took a large
mouthful. For the rest of the evening he sat there, ignoring his
wife when she timidly put her head around the door to tell him
his tea was ready. She went upstairs to find something to do that
would ensure her temporary seclusion.

Over an hour passed but he seldom moved except at intervals
to take a gulp of whisky. As he sat, he thought. His thought
processes were not very rapid but his mind turned bitterly as he
repeated the words: "Thou be better hadst thou never met with
me." These strangely phrased words seemed to have sunk into
his brain. They seemed familiar; he had heard them before. But
where? They brought his mother to mind. He remembered her
dimly. The village had called her the Cunning Woman and she
had been in demand for all sorts of cures, both for animals and

people. He had been a little boy at her death, when all the colour had gone out of his life. She had warned him of various people, especially the schoolmistress. She had, she said, an "evil eye". His careful avoidance of her and his wilful refusal to cooperate with her must have been largely responsible for his leaving school moderately illiterate. He could, when he bothered, understand bureaucratic jargon in government forms which he signed when absolutely necessary. But he resolutely avoided the written word, except for one book, which he had often read. His mother had left it to him, having been presented with it by the author herself.

He remembered the occasion. The author, another over-educated woman, had often come to see his mother, who had apparently helped her to write the book. These writing people often stole ideas from simple folk like his mother, and then put down the ideas in their own fancy words and became rich. The book had been about witches long ago. His mother had known all about witches. His gran had even been in competition with them. Some of the older villagers remembered her. He thought about this while he had another gulp. The whisky was mellowing him so he got up and went over to the shelf and rummaged for the book. He found it and took it back to his seat and began to leaf through it, as he had often done before.

The book was called *Devon Witches* and was a collection of anecdotes about local characters through the generations. But he didn't look at the title. He opened it and let it fall open where it chose. It fell open where an old match lay imbedded. He began to read.

He stared at the page for some considerable time until he began to understand the text. His large calloused hands held the book clumsily. His eyes fell upon a set of quotation marks and a sentence separated itself from the text. 'Thou be better hadst thou never met with me.'

As he syllablised the words slowly, the realisation of what he read hit him – hit him hard. He dropped the book as though it were red-hot. He sat shocked for a while, and then got up and blundered across the room to climb the stairs. He pulled open his bedroom door and slammed it behind him as though to shut something out. He hauled off his outer clothing and threw it across the room. Then he climbed into bed, ignoring his silent wife, and lay staring sightlessly at the ceiling. There came a silence over the house. Nothing moved, but out in the field a large hare sat up on its hind quarters and looked towards the farm house. Its nose twitched as though in amusement, and its eyes glared with malice. It sat still – it appeared to be concentrating. After a while it dropped on all fours and loped back across the field.

The following morning the farmer went to call his cows. As he worked in the shippon, his mind was obsessed with Mrs Trevisard. His insult in calling her a witch had only been due to his temper and his limited knowledge of women. His range of insults for a woman was generally obscene; he did not think of them in any other way and educated women were mostly outside his experience. The only really evil women he had any knowledge of were from his childish memories. These women were, in his mother's and grandmother's talk, witches. This was his only reason for so calling Mrs Trevisard. Her response and his literary discovery put his mind in a whirl. But the idea began to form. She had a power, for she had easily overawed him. Why was he frightened of her? No one else had ever frightened him, he convinced himself. How could she do it? Surely only if she had some unusual power. He thought about this as he prepared his next cow for the milking machine.

He slapped her into her bay and reached under her to take her teats. He squirted some milk onto the floor to loosen her up, and saw that it had some yellowish clots. He stared in surprise and tried again. The milk squirted sluggishly and again these buttery clots appeared. He splashed some milk onto his hand and tentatively tasted it. His head reared up, for it was surprisingly bitter. He ran his tongue over his lips and disgustedly spat. The milk left a sharp, sour taste in his mouth and he blinked in puzzlement. He rose up stiffly and collected a bucket from the wall alongside the shippon. He hand-milked the cow and half filled the bucket. Now the yellow lumps were very definite. He swirled the bucket and watched them float lazily around it. What was this? He looked at the cow with care. She seemed all right. Her eyes were bright and she stared back at him incuriously. But as he looked at her, the cow behind gave a heavy cough, threw up its head and vomited across the shed. The vomit struck the wall opposite with force. Again she coughed, seeming to suck her whole insides in, and again a lump of greenish vomit sped across and hit the wall with a violent splat. There came another cough from outside and all the cows seemed to be moving restlessly. They began to moo in a melancholy way. The farmer took up the bucket and pushed his way through the distressed herd to look at them and then stared into the bucket and moodily swished the contents around. He was puzzled. They appeared to be poisoned. He stood in the middle of the restless herd while they coughed and moved about stiffly in the foul yard. They held their heads out stiffly and as he watched, another coughed and spat at the floor. He threw the bucket down in exasperation, the contents spilling over the dung-bestrewn yard. He saw the lumps lie like small egg-yolks. He stamped on them and went back into the shippon with some decision in his stride.

He carefully handmilked the affected cow into some buckets and set them to one side. He pushed her out of the bay and continued to clear out the rest of his distressed herd, going often to the milk container to check its contents. The rest of the milk seemed quite satisfactory. When he had finished he turned the cattle out of the yard and into the field. There was no more vomiting. He leant on the gate and watched them, his face screwed up in concentration. They stood in the field, some grazing desultorily but most of them just standing. As he anxiously watched them, his eye was caught by a movement near the hedge. He turned to look and saw the hare sitting up. It also appeared to be examining the cattle. It turned to look at the farmer, gave him a long look and turned back to the cows. It turned again to the farmer and almost in amusement as well as triumph showed him its scut as it bounced back into the long grass beside the hedge and disappeared.

This appearance decided the farmer. He marched back to the farmhouse, kicked off his wellingtons and went into the kitchen. His wife was carefully peeling potatoes in the sink. He ignored her again and went straight through to his chair in the living room, and picked up the book that still lay where he had dropped it the night before.

He sat down and turned to the beginning of the book. He

wriggled himself deep into his chair and began to read. The book was divided into various parts. The first dealt with all sorts of Magic. The farmer's calloused finger slowly moved along the page, often pausing where the words were long or the sentences complicated. But he made certain he understood before reading on. Whenever he had read this book before he had merely skipped over anything that seemed incomprehensible. Now he examined the phrases like a scholar. He learnt that witches were capable of manipulating the powers of nature. They could turn this force or that to their will. He read of witches who could control the weather, fly through the air, cause love and hate, bring plague and even war. He also read of witches who could cause disease in an enemy's family, blight on his crops and murrain on his cattle. Here he paused and stuck his nose deep into the part dealing with animal sickness. There were many examples of witches' power to cause distress to animals. Here he read carefully. Cows appeared especially prone to a witch's malevolence. But the book was irritatingly unspecific. He paused and looked up to see his wife peering around the door, staring with surprise at her husband. To see him sitting in a chair, in the middle of the morning and especially to see him reading a book at such a time, seemed incredible. As their eyes met she bobbed back into the kitchen. He grunted and went back to his book. He flicked through some more pages.

He came to some drawings, which showed women with withered faces in tall hats. He ignored these and began to read the text. Here he discovered some details of the cult and the behaviour of these women. He read of their knowledge and their care of herbs. He read that they often gathered their herbs 'under cover of night not for concealment but because herbs required the moon for their power. Often a witch had to be naked or skyclad for the gathering.' This, he read, 'affected the potency of the herbs.' Here he paused and reread the passage, nodding his head in satisfaction.

He went through long lists of herbs and their properties. He read of Foxglove, Henbane, Deadly Nightshade, Mandrake, Thorn Apple, Aconite and Monkshood. He read how witches can cause miscarriages in women and impotence in men. The more he read, the more restless he became. Suddenly he became

galvanised into action. He rose out of his chair and hurried out
of the room to the back door and put on his boots. He crossed
the yard and entered the field opposite Mrs Trevisard's house.
He moved furtively across the grass to the hedge and walked
quietly along it to where he could see into her cottage. There he
crouched and watched. He peered through the burgeoning
leaves with a steady concentration. Nearly an hour passed
without him making a movement. The cottage lay quietly in the
sun. Occasionally a bird flew across his line of sight while others
rustled in the dead wood at the base of the hedge, but otherwise
nothing happened.

Eventually the silence was broken as the door of the cottage
opened and Mrs Trevisard came out. The farmer sank lower
behind his cover. Mrs Trevisard closed the door, leaving it
unlocked in the trusting rural fashion, and walked across to her
car, a small, shiny Metro. 'Trust her to have such a smart new
car!' he thought She climbed in and drove off with a very
masculine skirl of gravel and a decided turn of speed. As the car
disappeared into the trees and the engine faded away, the farmer
moved. He mounted the hedge and holding a young ash, vaulted
clumsily into the garden. He walked hastily to the door and let
himself in.

The front door led straight into the living room. It was a
large, airy spacious room, exquisite in its neatness and bright,
harmonising colours. One long wall was covered with large,
filled bookshelves; there were more books than he had ever seen
in anyone's home. But his eyes didn't linger on the décor or the
books. He was looking for something. His attention was caught
by a small folding table against the wall, under a niche. It was
covered with a red cloth on which stood two ornate candlesticks
with black candles in them. He noticed that they were half
burned away. In between the candles, lay a large, decorated knife
in front of a tall slender statuette. He moved closer, stepping
with exaggerated care. He picked up the figure and examined it
closely. It was carved out of a very dark wood; it was a tall,
naked man wearing antlers. Its face was crudely carved and
stared back at him with open, sightless eyes. He put it back
hurriedly and picked up the knife. It was in fact a dagger and
very beautifully made. It had an ornate handle, covered with

strange designs let into the ivory. It looked like foreign writing. He tapped his hand meditatively and looked into the niche. In it stood a tall silver chalice, shaped like a trophy. A prize, he thought, but it also was engraved with the same strange unreadable writing. He carefully replaced the knife, correcting its position so that it shouldn't look disturbed. He examined the rest of the room: in the fireplace, which was obviously never used for its original purpose – it was too clean and painted – there hung on an old firehook a large cast iron pot. Its black, matt surface gleamed like a huge malevolent eye. Nonetheless, it seemed to satisfy the farmer. Still his gaze kept searching the room. He walked, very carefully, over to a neat little escritoire under an elegant standard lamp. He opened it and found letters, bills, receipts and the usual clutter, all assembled together with bulldog clips. Such evidence of neatness and efficiency made him feel foolishly inept and clumsy. He opened the drawer below and found an unusual leather book. It had soft, worn covers. It had a hand-made look to it, well worn but not old. Beside it was a leather bag closed with a beaded draw-string. It looked full. He picked it up and pushed his finger into it. It opened and he peered in. There were some polished stones, some dried leaves, a little paper packet of what appeared to be earth or dust. There were some old fashioned farriers' nails, a rabbit's foot, a feather, some uncommon coins and a packet of hair. He examined this weird collection, but felt he didn't want to touch them. He pulled the string tight and put the bag back. He carefully took the book out; under it there lay a silver chain. It was the silver necklace she had worn yesterday. It had a simple crescent moon hanging from it. He turned back to the book.

He opened it and found the thick ragged-edged pages were covered by a minute, black but very neat handwriting. It was very difficult to read and it didn't look like English. It appeared to be set out like a diary. As he thumbed through the pages, he saw that at least half of the book was unused. The heading of the last page used was BELTANE. This he could read as it was in capital letters. But it meant nothing to him.

He put the book back, his face creased with the effort of thought. He still seemed unsatisfied. He craned his neck up the staircase, but hesitated to go up. He turned back into the room, crossed the floor and opened another door. He entered the kitchen. It was small and very neat. He saw the small, shining stove, the clean, clear surfaces, and the many glass jars displaying their contents, and the ceramic pots that didn't. Everything in sight had a decorative quality; nothing was purely functional. The room gave the farmer his confidence back: this kitchen was very different from his own, nonetheless he understood its function. He stepped across the room, grinding his feet into the floor with his old aggressive certainty. He stood in the middle of the floor and looked around him. A sudden noise made him jump and cringe. It was only the fridge motor starting up. But it took away his newly acquired confidence. He hurried towards the back door. Here he paused, his eyes lit up. He reached into the corner beside the door and seized a broom. It was the old fashioned type. It was made of reed that was bound to the handle with an intricate pattern. Like everything else it was more decorative than functional. But this looked brand new. It obviously hadn't been used. He picked it up, rather gingerly, and examined it with an intense scrutiny. It seemed to confirm his impressions, and in contrast to his previous timidity he thrust it back and strode out of the house, slamming the door behind him. He scrambled over the hedge, clumped across the field and back into his own yard.

He went straight into his barn, drove out his Landrover and rattled out of the farm yard. He left his wife staring forlornly out of the kitchen window behind him.

His Landrover bucketed along the road towards the local market town. He stared straight ahead, hunched over the wheel as he drove the few miles to the town. He came into the main square and parked in front of the town hall, got down and hastened away, leaving the door to swing closed behind him. He headed for the market, where the library was. Entering the building, he seemed at a loss; he felt large and incongruously scruffy in this clean modern library filled with bookish quiet. Sheepishly he waited at the desk while an elderly man talked earnestly about railway lines. The farmer listened: this man was gathering information on the old railway that had once run into the town: he wanted timetables and route maps. The woman at the desk, trim and tidy, listened and made suggestions; they both behaved as though they had all the time in the world. Eventually the farmer gave up and walked away to look among the shelves, when, turning a corner, he came upon someone he knew. It was the local vet: not a man he thought highly of, and one he would normally avoid, but these were unusual circumstances. He moved alongside and grunted a "Good Morning". The vet looked up from his book and an incredulous smile appeared on his ruddy face.

"Good Lord! Hullo, what are you doing here?"

"I'm looking for information on witchcraft, folklore and things. Where do I look?" the farmer mumbled awkwardly.

His companion's face beamed with delight.

"Of course. You're following after your mam. Isn't it a bit late for you to start being Cunning?" The joke seemed to convulse the vet as much as it embarrassed the farmer.

"Well, where do I look, then?" Rumbling with laughter, the vet took the farmer by the arm and led him to some other bookshelves.

"Look through some of them and you'll find out how to make yourself a love poppet." The guide laughed at his own joke so loud that the heads of various browsers came up out of their books and looked at them with disapproval. The farmer was nonplussed, so to divert attention he reached for the nearest book. It was a large paperback. He glared at the title, which said *Witches*. As he looked at it, he soon forgot his humilation and became absorbed. The cover had a large, gaudy circle, centering a goat and a nude woman. Around these figures was lettering, including the months of the year. Above May was the word 'Beltane' in old lettering. He opened the book and found in it many bright pictures. He thumbed through it, fascinated. He saw a picture of a priest-like man holding a candle and wearing robes decorated with goats. He saw lurid pictures of women on fire or hanging by the neck. There were nude women in all sorts of strange conditions, women attached to cats or turning into all sorts of animals. He saw a hare that stared at him with an unfocused malevolent look. He saw toads, crows and bats.

He came across a drawing and various objects that pertained to witches. Here he stopped and read the text carefully: 'A Witch has a wand made of a sacred wood; an Athame, a decorated

dagger; a Bolline, a white handled knife for ritual purposes; a
Cord or Cingulam, which she wears about her waist; a Cauldron
and a Chalice. For her personal adornment she wears moons, sea
shells or blue stones. She carries a Conjure Bag containing
thirteen charms. She has her wand and always her Book of
Shadows.' He read on, shaking with excitement: 'A cloak, a
girdle, gloves and pointed shoes. A garter, a crown and of
course her broom. She is usually accompanied by her familiar.
This is usually a cat or a rabbit but many animals, reptiles and
even insects have been recorded. It is said that a Witch is capable
of taking the shape of many animals: wolves, cats, dogs, cows
and hares.'

This last caused the reader to stop and look carefully. He
stood as though frozen. Other readers stopped and stared at him
but he seemed oblivious. Then he put the book down and
almost ran to the door. He jostled aside those in his way, leaving
many staring after him in surprise. He rushed out to his
Landrover and climbed in. Its familiar filth seemed to restore
him. He sat a long time, looking without seeing and breathing
deeply. Then having calmed down, he left the vehicle and
walked across to the pub. He now was more his normal self. He
pushed his way to the bar and ordered a pint of bitter and when
this had been sunk, he looked around him. All appeared normal.
The air was filled with tobacco smoke and general chatter. There
was no one he knew. But then he wasn't the social type. He
ordered a large pasty and a refill of his pint and took them over
to a quiet empty corner seat and sat, drank, ate and thought.

He was there a long time and did not leave until the pub
closed. He walked down the street with a determined air. He
went into the Ironmonger's and purchased a packet of 4.10
cartridges. With these he came back to his car. He climbed in
and drove home.

His fingers drummed on the steering wheel and he sat
hunched over the wheel as though urging the vehicle forward.
He eyes shone and his jaw moved as though in silent speech.
Nonetheless he drove slowly and arrived home as the evening
began to draw in. His cows were awaiting him in the yard. They
gave every impression of being healthy and were no longer
uncomfortable. But he carefully hand milked the cow that had

given the thick infected milk separately. There were no further signs of sickness.

He came out into the yard. Now the light was almost gone. The evening was still and outside the ring of the only just necessary light, the world seemed silent. He leant on the gate, staring and waiting. It didn't take very long, and he gave a sigh of satisfaction. There was the hare. It rose up onto its hindquarters and looked at him. It hesitated and seemed unsure. He glared across at it and his growls changed to a deep rumbling laughter, deep in this throat. It was the hare that was disconcerted; it took a pace back and looked at him. It paused. Again the farmer laughed quietly and then threw back his head with a wild, maniacal laugh. The hare dropped onto its four legs and disappeared quickly towards Mrs Trevisard's cottage. The farmer roared again his insane laugh and turned back towards his house. Now he almost danced as he tucked the box of cartridges under his arm. He grinned at his startled wife and went straight past her into the living-room and began to search through drawers in an old chest. He hurled out the contents, then with a sudden neigh of triumph rose to his full height clutching in his huge hand a small silver spoon. He was chuckling with glee as he turned to go out, leaving the drawers hanging open.

His wife, who had watched this extraordinary scene, said: "What are you doing? That's my christening spoon. You can't have that! It was my gran's! It's pure silver!"

He laughed heartily, as though her comment was just what he wanted to hear. She came forward tentatively and tried to take it from him. He struck out at her and she leapt back in fear, her hands flying protectively to her face.

"Just the thing to lay the bitch," he barked, and still laughing, left the room.

His wife stood for a moment wringing her hands, her face gathered up in a grimace. Then she went back to the kitchen and peered out of the window, through the darkness, towards the light in the workshop window. For some moments she stood staring out, wiping the sink mechanically, and her whole body trembled. Then she put by her cloth and her apron, opened the door timidly, tiptoed across the yard to the shed, and peeped furtively in at the window.

Her husband had a Calor gas ring blazing, and on it an old
glue pot, out of which stuck the handle of her silver spoon. She
moaned slightly in protest but made no move. He picked up a
bucket and, with a glance at the spoon, came out into the yard
to fill it at a nearby tap. For a moment the water roared. Then
he turned off the tap, and he was still chuckling to himself as he
carried the full bucket back into the shed. If he saw his wife, he
took no notice of her. He put the bucket down and went over
to the glue pot. He carefully touched the top of the spoon and
immediately whipped away his hand with a curse. But the pain
merely seemed to amuse him. He watched closely as the handle
moved and sank a little. It then collapsed into the pot. He stared
in delight. His whole body was hunched over the stove. The
light of the gas illuminated his face in a theatrically diabolic way.
His eyes gleamed and his ruddy face shone. He took up a piece
of wire and gently stirred the pot. As he lifted the wire, the
lower part shone and gleamed with an extraordinary brightness.

This seemed to satisfy him. He turned off the gas and with his
hands protected with layers of sacking, he slowly picked up the
glue pot. With a sudden, deft swing, he poured the contents into
the bucket at his feet. The silvery blob hit the water in an
explosive hiss, clouds of steam wreathed up towards his face,
exaggerating the threatricality of the scene. He stared down,
gloating, his bulbous eyes now almost frenzied with excitement.
He bent down and carefully put his hand into the bucket. What
he found seemed to satisfy him and with a contented grunt he
turned towards the box of cartridges. He wiped his hand and
carefully selected one. He examined it and then with his penknife
he edged up and away the cardboard wad that held in the shot
and the charge. He carefully shook out the contents, examined
the pellets in his hand and put them on the work bench. Taking
another cartridge, he did the same thing, but this time he
emptied the powder into the first cartridge. He then put the full
cartridge to one side. Bending down to the bucket, he removed
the shining sphere of silver, which he held up to the light.

He then tried to fit the sphere into the loaded cartridge.
Where it didn't fit he marked it and then began to work on it
with a file. He worked quickly and with a craftsmanship that was
surpising in such a coarse and clumsy man.

His wife watched timorously for a while and then returned, puzzled, to her kitchen.

The farmer came back to the house to collect a single-barrelled 4.10 shotgun from above the fireplace. It was of a very ancient design and very rusty. He rubbed off the cobwebs and dust. Then he broke it open. He blew down the barrel, closed it and pulled the trigger, watching the hammer fall. He took it back to the shed and cleaned it, removing as much rust as he could. He oiled it generously and moved all the working parts as much as possible. When he was convinced that all was working as smoothly as it could, he inserted the rebuilt cartridge. He tested the extractor: it worked. He hefted the gun in his hand and sighted it across the room. Then he broke it open again, removing the cartridge, which he placed in his pocket. He then re-examined the gun and began to clean it yet again. He repeated all his manoeuvres with precision and care. All the while, he hummed to himself tunelessly, in high good humour. He took the gun back to the farmhouse. As he came through the kitchen, his good spirits so infected his wife that she dared to ask him what he was doing. She was startled by his roar of joviality.

"Can you jug a hare?" He rumbled with laughter. "I am going to get a hare for Sunday's dinner." This seemed to amuse him immoderately. His wife didn't dare to ask more, especially why he had taken her spoon. Nor could she bring herself to ask why he had made a silver bullet.

He did his evening chores in almost joyous abandon, often breaking into noisy guffaws. His cows seemed to be taken aback with his gaiety, as he turned them out into the field. He was obviously very satisfied with himself.

When he came into the house for his tea, he sat down and ate it with unexpected conviviality. He even commented on the food. His smiles and laughter again emboldened his wife to ask what his plans were. He merely grinned and said that he would sort out that Mrs Trevisard.

"She don't know that I know." This seemed to amuse him again and he rose from the table and went back into the living room and again ensconced himself in his chair. He took up the book and began to read.

He had brought in the shotgun and had placed it beside the chair. He kept patting it and chuckling to himself.

He opened the book where it had originally fallen open, and read of a couple of Dartmouth sailors who in the 1640s had crossed the Moor from Barnstaple. They had run into a woman who, they were unaware, was a local witch. They had tried to proposition her. In the ensuing argument they had drunkenly struck her, when she had said: "Thou be better hadst thou never met with me." He read on to discover that their ship had foundered at sea with few survivors.

He closed the book slowly and stared unseeingly at the wall. His face seemed alight with an almost hypnotic intensity. His hand reached back and fumbled for the gun. It found it and drew it to him. He brought it out in front of him and pointed it at the wall. He sighted and pulled the trigger. As the hammer clicked down, he sighed deeply and sensuously. He sat still, fondling the gun almost affectionately. Then he rose from his chair, gathered up the gun, cradling it in his arms, and walked out of the room past his gaping wife. He took no notice of her, his mood now sombre, and went to the door almost somnambulistically, ignoring his boots and padded across the muck-filled yard in his stockinged feet. He reached the gate and opened it. He held the gun high, and on the other side took the cartridge out of his pocket. He unwrapped it from the handkerchief, letting the handkerchief fall. It floated to the ground like a ghostly, white, fluttering bird. He loaded the gun and carefully closed the chamber. He folded the hammer to 'safe'. Then he strode stolidly across the field towards Mrs Trevisard's cottage.

At the hedge he turned and moved along it until he was opposite the front door. There he crouched down, shuffled himself into comfort and froze into immobility.

There was a light on in the window, casting a slight, warm, yellow glow across the small lawn and the paved path that ran in a straight line to the front door. As he sat and waited the shadows deepened and lengthened and now despite the light from the window, the moon gave everything a cold ominous look.

The night was almost still: there was barely wind enough to moan and sigh softly in the trees. The moon glowed silver and dark grey clouds tumbled across the sky, varying the light, so that everything seemed to be undulating, as though it were controlling its breathing – as though it were preparing to squeeze an aimed shot.

A shadow moved across the yellow square of window and another light, on the other side of the door, blinked on. The scene was transformed: the little area in front of the door was lit up. A beam of light shone down the path from a small square patch of glass in the front door. It lit up the path, showing the irregularity of the paving stones in high relief.

There came no movement from the farmer. He stared across at the door, while the extra light glittered on his eyes. Slowly his head moved and he began to search around him. The light came and went on his eyes as they roved the garden.

The flickering of his eyes stopped as his ears caught the slightest of sounds, a small shuffling outside the range of light. It came again. Then slowly the hare came lolloping across the grass into the area of light. It paused on the periphery, crouched and then, as if suspecting something, rose up on its hind-legs and sniffed the air. Its nose trembled delicately as it sniffed the night smells; it hesitated and dropped back onto its forelegs, paused undecided and then hopped across the slim border bed and onto the path. The animal sat looking towards the door, clearly silhouetted in the light.

The farmer moved silently; slowly his gun came down and began to bear on the hare.

At that moment the door opened and the light splashed across the path; the hare was galvanised into movement and flashed away as the gun roared. As the echoes died, a long, thin, wavering scream was heard.

BY chance some unexpected guests of Mrs Trevisard, arriving later that night, came across the scene.

Slumped across the doorstep was the body of Mrs Trevisard, shot through the breast. The farmer was soon found, lying in the hedge with most of his head blown away. He lay across the split, exploded chamber of his shotgun.

The rest of the night was filled with the comings and goings of cars and ambulances.

The police and the coroner came to these conclusions:

Mrs Trevisard had been shot with a home-made silver bullet.

This bullet had been made and shot by the farmer, who had fired towards the door of the cottage. His bullet had ricochetted off the path and hit Mrs Trevisard.

The farmer's shotgun, unable to withstand the extra charge and the solid bullet, had split with the explosion and killed the farmer.

The farmer's wife confirmed the animosity her husband bore towards their neighbour, and the making of the bullet, but could give no reasonable motive for this apparent murder.

The coroner decided, in the case of Mrs Trevisard, that she had died by Unlawful Killing; in the case of the farmer, by Accidental Death. No further action was appropriate.

The hare was never seen again.

The Tower

Robin A Harward

IT was a still evening as the Wing-Commander sat on his friends' patio looking out over the tranquil estuary towards the Devon hills, while the ice in his gin and tonic clinked comfortably. There stood the tower: it had often caught his eye, jutting out against the horizon. As he looked at it an idea formed in his mind, and it remained with him the whole of the evening.

The conversation at dinner was lively and amusing, between old friends with whom he was totally at ease.

The last few months had been excessively trying and he was mentally and physically exhausted, to the point where he had needed medical attention. He had been told to rest and do nothing for at least ten days before reporting for another physical and mental examination, so he had inevitably thought of going to the Hardings. He had been at school with Richard and had known Julia before Richard had met her. Since their marriage, their house, overlooking the lovely estuary, had been his home from home, where he was always welcome.

Richard and Julia were both practising doctors and worked hard. He was used to staying there alone and pottering about the house when they were at work. When he stayed with them he was made responsible for planning and cooking the evening meal, and he felt this was his rent. He was childishly pleased when his hosts declared that they never ate so well when he wasn't there.

On this visit his mind instantly reverted to its main pre-occupation: his medical examination. It worried him. He tried not to think about it, but he was aware that the rest of his life depended on it. He couldn't imagine what he would do if he couldn't fly again and was told to retire. He mustn't think about that now, but his efforts to join in the Hardings' family life were more forced than usual and he felt somehow distanced from it.

What he needed was something to do. Something trivial and interesting that would occupy and not overtax his mind.

Today he had got up late, dawdled over breakfast, seen his

hosts off to their joint surgery, washed up and read the paper. He had then pottered through a recipe book, listed the ingredients for the meal of his choice and wandered down to the delicatessen in the village to collect whatever the well-stocked kitchen didn't contain. He had prepared the meal with his usual meticulousness, chopping and measuring and mixing until it reached the cooking stage. He had then placed it all in the automatic oven, enjoying setting the dials with an engineer's enthusiasm. Then he settled himself on the patio with his gin and tonic and awaited their return.

LATER that night, as he lay in bed, his idea came back to him. He had decided that he would go to have a look at that tower. He had often seen it on the horizon and wondered about it in a desultory fashion. The Hardings knew nothing of it when he had asked them. They assumed it to be a Victorian folly. As one had to drive all round the estuary to get anywhere near it, and the area it was in had only a few farms, and no patients in their practice, they had never seen it closer.

So the Wing-Commander had come to the decision that he would go to look at it and see what information he could find out about it. All his life he had been a man of decision and now, having been reminded of the idea, he got out of bed, went down to the hall and opened the drawer in which he knew he would find the Hardings' maps. He found the right one, spread it out on the floor, angled a nearby light over it and knelt down to examine it. He found the relevant wood across the estuary and in the middle of it was the cryptic message 'tower'. With a grunt of satisfaction he left the map, turned out the light and went back to bed. Now his decision was confirmed, he quickly went to sleep.

The following morning he told the Hardings that he had decided to drive round the estuary to have a look at the tower. He would climb to the top. Richard laughed, and told him to plant a flag on it so they could toast his discovery before dinner. Julia, more practical, asked if he wanted to take a picnic lunch. But he decided that a pub lunch would be easier and the conversation moved on to the dinner he would prepare that evening. He insisted that he would be back in plenty of time to cook it. Richard told him that he had two bottles of a very nice Medoc that were awaiting a deserving meal to complement them. This reminded him of a certain recipe that he wanted to try so he promised them something rather special. The friends parted in good spirits.

The Wing-Commander washed up the breakfast, collected the map, got into his car and set off with a pleasurable feeling of expectation and purpose. As he drove he wondered about follies and the world that had enabled one to be wealthy enough to indulge a whim durable enough to outlast oneself, and to give employment with no consideration of profit. His school history had taught him to deplore such inequality. But he couldn't help feeling that he would like to employ the unemployed to do something just for fun.

He had soon driven through the suburbs of the little port at the top of the estuary, crossed the bridge and reached the other side. He became aware of his English insularity and was amused at the sense of having crossed a boundary. Although the lanes were as narrow and as winding as on the other side and the architecture and landscape were identical, he did feel that he was somewhere different. No wonder, he laughed to himself, that Devonians are aware as they cross the Tamar that they have left England and entered the Duchy of Cornwall. Until now this idea had always seemed ridiculous to him.

He changed down to bottom gear to climb a steep little hill in front of him, unable to see anywhere because of the high hedges, covered in summer growth, on either side. Then he stopped in a gateway and climbed out with the map to check his bearings.

As he looked over the gate and down to the estuary, he felt relaxed and at peace. He enjoyed a leisurely look, amusing himself by searching for familiar landmarks on the other side, his side. At last he found the Hardings' house. It was almost lost in the trees and was only recognisable by its green-tiled roof. He felt almost certain that he could see the patio. If he was correct, the tower should be up on his right. With some effort he climbed the gate and then with the aid of a friendly and convenient oak, scrambled onto the hedge. He felt disconcerted that such a little exertion had so exhausted him. He recovered his breath and peered through the branches, to see the tower beyond him. It rose up through the trees, covered with ivy, much taller than he had expected and somehow gothic and rather ominous. It was tall and narrow, and the ivy covering it was interspersed with little lancet windows that glowered at him like eyes frowning out under heavy brows. Its top was crenellated and its outline blurred by the heavy growth.

He realised that he was unlikely to be able to drive any nearer so when he had climbed down carefully from his perch he locked up the car and set off up the road to find a way through the opposite hedge. He soon found a gap, haphazardly filled with barbed wire and rickety stakes. He negotiated this obstacle and then started through the head-high bracken, in the direction in which he had seen the tower.

It was a steep climb; the ground was overgrown and much cut up by cattle, and by the time he arrived at the top he was lathered with sweat and panting heavily. The high bracken had prevented him seeing ahead but his navigational instincts had been correct. There, in a clearing of brown windswept grass, was his tower. It loomed up ahead of him louring over him, immense and challenging. He walked towards it and circled round it. There were windows all round it and at the back a small low door. It was a wooden door that appeared to be locked, with a board nailed across it from door-post to door-post. As he felt the door he suddenly felt frightened. There was no reason why he should; he looked round him: there was nothing there, just the wind sighing through the grass; but somehow everything seemed to be holding its breath.

As he felt or rather tested the board across the door it fell away, its nails rusted through. He pushed at the door and it held but when he tried the rusty handle he felt it reluctantly and ungraciously turn, so that the door was loose in his hand. He hesitated, still weighed down by this feeling of fear, which made his hair prickle. He felt that he was being watched and again he looked around him. He could see nobody; nor was there anywhere anyone could be, unless they were crouching in the bracken. If they were hiding from him, he reasoned, they couldn't be dangerous. But he was a man who was accustomed to overcoming fear; indeed, fear was a challenge in itself: if you were frightened, then press on but use your fear to increase your caution. So he gently pushed the door. Reluctantly it creaked open, pushing back the leaves that had piled up in a sticky, wet compost behind it.

In front of him was a small, stone flagged area that enabled the door to open and from which steps wound up a narrow spiral staircase. The only light came from the open door and illuminated the stairs as far as he could see. Pulling himself together and deliberately defying his unnatural fear, he stooped under the lintel and went in. He began climbing the stairs and as he turned he saw that his way was lit by one of the small lancet windows.

The stairs were rough and uneven. The place smelt damp and dead. But there was more. He was aware that he didn't want to go on. He realised that he was more frightened than he had ever been since a child. He was more frightened than he had been when he had made his first parachute jump. He remembered that cold, wet, dispiriting day. He had known then that his fears were typical. He couldn't back out in front of his fellow officers, although he realised that they must all have been feeling the same. Indeed, they had all said so afterwards. But then there was the comradeship of his fellow sufferers and the firm, encouraging tact of his instructors. Here, now, he was alone. He had never felt so alone. He could turn round and go away. No one would know. He could tell the Hardings that he hadn't felt like it, so he hadn't bothered to climb to the top. They were doctors and knew all about him. They would understand. That was the rub; that was it; they were worried that he was cracking up. They hadn't said so, but their kindness and consideration had told him so. Could he really turn round and walk away from . . . what? From nothing! – except a vague superstitious fear that he wasn't wanted.

A man who flashed across the sky in a multi-million jet fighter – the glamour figure of his time – could he allow himself just to walk away?

As he paused on the rough stairs to lean against the uneven wall, he knew that he couldn't. He must snap out of it, and see what there was to see. He would discuss his unreasoning fear with Richard and Julia this evening over dinner. They would laugh at it and explain how stress and exhaustion could play strange tricks with a man's mind. They would show concern. Richard would recommend a double dose of his favourite malt whisky and that would be that.

So he continued climbing. It was uncomfortable as the stairs were too narrow and the treads too short. But the light from the windows was just sufficient. So up he went. As he came round the next circle, he bent down to look out of the little window and gaze across the estuary, which looked so peaceful and unruffled. The water had the smoothness of marble and was dotted with the brightly-coloured sails of apparently motionless little sailing dinghies. In fact everything was curiously still. But on he went, his hands on either side of the wall. He used the rough projecting stones as handholds and indeed began to feel that he was rock climbing rather than going up a stairway. He climbed slowly round again. His thighs were beginning to feel the pressure and he was tiring. Never mind, he would soon be at the top, it couldn't be far now. He had circled at least four times. He pressed on, stopping at each window, glancing out, more for a breather than the view. Each time the view seemed the same, curiously motionless with nothing changed. The smooth expanse of water, browning where it was shallow, and the rough velvet of the trees had a hypnotic quality.

His fears had gone with the effort and concentration of climbing. He must be nearly there now. But the steps still spiralled upward. His thighs were now aching and his knees creaked at the effort. So he stopped at the next window, awkwardly turned round and sat down. When he was moderately comfortable he looked out of the window. It was still the same view. It somehow unnerved him. The Hardings' house seemed to be looking at him but with an unseeing look. He felt that it wasn't seeing him, as if he wasn't there. He chuckled rather miserably at his foolish thought. But then he realised that the view was indeed still. It was like looking at a picture. But that was impossible. He listened, but he heard nothing; no wind nor the distant drone of aeroplane, tractor or road traffic, nor an occasional burst of birdsong. There was no sound except his own breathing and the rapid knock of his heart, which was racing. Perhaps he was attempting too much; after all he wasn't well, he was ill. The tower was uncomfortable and very cramped. Why was he going up it at all? There was no need, it was of no importance. Some foolish rich man had built it here to satisfy a selfish whim. No planning authority would allow it today. To think of the poor labourers lugging these heavy stones up the hill made him indignant. He imagined them working on precarious old-fashioned scaffolding for a mere pittance. No, he was wasting his time.

But to hell with that, he thought; he had set himself a challenge, a simple task to go up a little tower. Surely he wasn't so run down and feeble that he couldn't do that! And anyway, he had all day. He could take his time.

So he got up laboriously and turned around and continued up the stairs. The next window lit his path. Ahead were the same steps; worn, uneven and narrow. On he went. His hands were now on the steps in front of him. He continued climbing on all fours. Sweat was running down his neck. His hair, where it was rather too long, was now soaked and uncomfortable. His eyebrows seemed to be failing in their duty and his eyes were stinging with his sweat. But almost as an automaton he carried on up.

He stopped suddenly. What the hell was he doing? He must have come far enough. He stared out of the window and saw the same view. He seemed no higher. He glanced at his watch and to his horror he realised that he had been climbing for at least forty minutes. He couldn't have! What time had he started? He couldn't remember. He had left the house at ten. He had driven to the tower, which couldn't have taken more than forty minutes. His walk to the tower had taken another twenty. So he must have started climbing at about eleven o'clock. It was now eleven-forty. But then he had hesitated, hung about pausing at the windows, so perhaps he had been climbing for only twenty minutes. Even so, he ought to have reached the top. Somewhat puzzled and confused, he got up and continued climbing. He made a sudden determined burst and circled past three windows. Then he stopped, exhausted and angry. This was damn silly. Here he was sick and tired and forcing himself up a difficult climb, to no purpose. He must pull himself together and climb down. He had seen the view, so what was there to climb for? He wasn't a little boy trying to prove himself. He didn't lack guts.

Damn it! – he had medals to prove it. So he leant against the wall. But the wall didn't seem to want to make him comfortable and he couldn't relax in this cramped space. With deliberation, he began to control his breathing, and presently he felt better. Nonetheless, he wasn't an idiot, and it would be better to start going down. He would take some measurements from the bottom and do some mathematics to see how high the tower really was. And perhaps tomorrow, as it was Saturday, Richard and Julia would come along. They could take a picnic and come properly prepared. A gin would help them all up these blasted stairs. So he persuaded himself that he wasn't giving up. He climbed to his feet to begin to go down. Standing up and looking down, the stairs seemed horrifyingly steep and he felt a touch of vertigo. But he swallowed hard and began his descent.

Climbing down was more difficult then climbing up. His feet were too large for the stairs and the worn steps seemed far more slippery than before. He ignored the windows and concentrated on what he was doing. He realised that he was blotting out his mind. This was a phrase he used to describe the concentration required for some dicey operation when he would verbalise his instructions to his body. He knew that he was desparately trying to eliminate the frantic strivings of his imagination. It was absurd to think that the tower was hostile to him; it was merely an awkward climb. It was obviously no steeper than it had been when he climbed up. It just seemed so. He was now so tired that he paused, turned over and continued on all fours, like a child coming down stairs. He felt with his foot for the next step and slowly put his weight on it. It was much slower, but it seemed easier. Although he couldn't see his feet, he could lie down on his stomach occasionally and draw breath. So he went slowly on: a few steps down and then a rest, when he was on his belly in the dust on the stairs, with sweaty face resting on the dank stone. He knew that he was near the end of his tether and was aware of his fear. He could taste it, acrid and sour on the back of his throat. His breath rasped hot and thick. He had given up smoking two years earlier and after the first six months had felt no further need of it. Now among his other concerns, he was aware that he desperately needed a cigarette. His head was swimming and the sweat pricked his eyeballs. He paused to wipe it away. As he raised his hands he saw the grit and dust stuck to the sweat. There was blood on the knuckles. His face was running wet and he felt runnels of sweat trickling and tickling inside his shirt.

This was too ridiculous. He felt anger again at his weakness, at giving in to his foolish fear. He had given in to it all day. He would take a good long rest and then go up and finish the job. But he hadn't realised that he was so weak. Yet he knew that he was tough. Damn it, he wouldn't have got to his present rank and position if he wasn't!

What was at the top? He remembered as a boy climbing the bell tower at his local church and how excited he had been. He remembered the small door that had let him out on to the roof, the awe that he had felt at staring out over his own village, how different the view had looked, and the majesty of the aerial view that was now so familiar yet never mundane. He remembered how he had been able to see over walls that even on his bicycle he hadn't seen over and how he had examined the private back gardens of houses he knew well from the front. He remembered how he had looked down on top of a bird as it flew below him and knew that one day he would be a bird. Everything familiar had taken on a new look. He had stayed on the roof for so long that his parents, who had taken one look at the stairway and decided against climbing it, had become worried. His father had come up to collect him and berate him for not hearing their calls. But that door had had a padlock. The vicar had given his father the key. That was how he had got up. Perhaps this tower had a locked door! Perhaps he was struggling for nothing.

As he lay there remembering his childhood, he decided that he was middle-aged, too old to go climbing towers. He ought to go down. Perhaps he could come another time, to try again.

He again dragged himself up onto his toes, knees and elbows, and continued down. He began counting the stairs. He was surprised to hear himself counting aloud. He soon realised that as he had begun to count in the middle of the climb there was no point in doing it. So he stopped and continued down slowly step by step.

The windows circled past him. He seldom paused now to look at the view. It was always the same. The view gave no indication of a decrease in height; he seemed always neither higher nor lower than before. He was sure that he remembered windows on all sides of the tower. But that seemed so long ago. Why did he always get the same view? The tower had been wide enough to walk slowly round, yet now he was circling endlessly within his own length. Endlessly, that was the word.

He felt he was going 'round the twist', as it was aptly called. His mind revolved around the staircase and his head hammered. He had to keep on going to get out of this bloody tower. The Bloody Tower. He began to intone remembered fragments of the famous monologue. He lay on the stairs for a few moments shouting and laughing hysterically.

God, this won't do. He must compose himself. He clung to the stairs and drew long shuddering breaths while gradually his breathing eased. He licked his lips and tasted salt; not just sweat he grimly realised, but tears too.

As he moved on, letting his body slide over the steps and slip on down, he felt the rough projections catch him and as he winced he slipped and cracked his shin on the step edge. Was it possible to circle for ever in this tower? Could these fantasy chaps have something? He had read a few science fictions or fantasies and they had seemed absurd to a practical down-to-earth chap like himself. But could one get into time or space warps? Could he be trapped in some parallel universe?

Christ! What was he thinking now? If he didn't watch it, he really would go round the bend. The absurdity of the phrase now struck him and he began giggling, shouting, "Round the bend, round the bend."

He tried to move on again, but his muscles had stiffened, and to move was agony. He brought his arm slowly up to his face and as he stared at his grimy hands he saw his watch. Two forty five! My God! He shook his wrist and listened to the watch. It ticked quietly, efficiently and mockingly at him.

He hauled himself up and went up another stair. He wondered if he was going up or down. Somehow it didn't seem to matter as long as he kept going. 'Press on regardless' was what his motto had been, 'press on regardless'.

His foot slipped and he slid back; he scrabbled to stop himself but his body gained momentum. Every one of his bodily projections seemed to hit the edges of the steps; his elbows, knees, ribs, chin, and face. As he cascaded down the steps, striking out with his arms and legs to try to stop his progress he banged, scraped, and tore at the steps. The drumming of his body began to batter him into unconsciousness. The walls seemed to whirl about him and he seemed to be in a waterfall of stairs when all became suddenly dark.

THE teenage couple who found him at the bottom of the tower thought, in the modern suburban way, that he had been mugged. They quickly got help and he was taken to hospital. Most of his injuries were superficial grazes and bruises but the doctors were worried about his underlying condition. Richard and Julia were able to explain his previous medical record which alerted the doctors, and it was then that they diagnosed a heart attack.

When the Wing-Commander was able to talk coherently again and had explained his story, a further mystery was revealed, for the tower had had an iron grille put across the staircase a few feet from the bottom many years before, when the landowner had finally decided against maintaining it, and the staircase had began to disintegrate.

It was a long convalescence but the Wing-Commander, although he didn't fly again, went back to the service with no disability other than a reluctance to go up stairs where he couldn't see the top.

Chellew's Whistle

William Garnett

"KARLA," Janet's mother would say to the au pair, "be a sweet angel and take the children out into the park."

But what Janet liked best was to tiptoe into her father's work room – if nobody headed her off and he hadn't locked the door – and watch him blowing fire onto a piece of silver, or dipping it with his tweezers into a bubbling pan. Or he might be setting a jewel in a ring, or mending a clasp on a bracelet, or he might be deep in talk with a client who had brought some piece of work for him to do. If she was as quiet as a mouse he would sometimes let her stay; but at other times, without even looking up from his work he would suddenly shout: "Karla, come and take these brats off me!"

It was on such an occasion, when Karla was taking Janet and her little brother Brendan for a walk in Plymouth's Central Park, that she first saw Chellew. It was just a glimpse: he stood with hands cupped to mouth, so that his old coat spread wide like a cloak, while a couple of back street kids no bigger than Brendy stood watching. What was he doing? – warming his fingers? but it was July. Calling someone? But no sound came – only the rustling of the trees in the wind.

The second time she saw him he was sitting leaning on a park bench being scolded by a woman in a shawl who stood shaking her umbrella at him. Karla, wheeling Brendy in his push chair – for which he was far too big – had taken another turning off the path, and Janet, lagging behind, stood watching the scene as the old man turned up his palms and raised his eyebrows, shrugging his shoulders under his loose coat and shaking his broad head slowly. She took in those thick eyebrows, that were a shade darker grey than the silvery hair that escaped from the sides of the crumpled cap, and the eyes sunken beneath them almost as if he had been blind, that held a secret light in the rugged old face, contrasting with the sharp featured shrewish woman. She caught only the words: "A'll teach ee to intermeddle, Sam Chellew! Gaffer give it me with his own hands, didn't he?" And here the

89

woman choked off, aware of young ears listening. She bent to hiss something in his face, and with a final shake of the umbrella made off down the path. Only then had he glanced up at the child standing there, and smiled confidingly at her.

She came forward and with the directness which was the bane of her elders, asked "Is that your wife?" (The question was a natural one. Her own parents, Eric and Phillida, broke off just like this when interrupted in a row: often she thought she and Brendy were sent out into the park so that they might quarrel in peace.)

The old man shook his head with a laugh – at least, she couldn't be sure if he were laughing or crying – his face puckered up and for a moment she felt a pang of remorse for her directness with this pathetic old man. But the next moment he looked her straight in the eye and said: "If y'ever do volks a good turn, don' ee ever expect to git thanked vor ut. Mind what I zay, young Miss."

She stood before him puzzled at this talk of doing good turns – him, a tramp. What could he do? So, giving him her most searching stare, she said "Who would ever thank you anyway?"

"Ah," he said, laughing at her again. "Y'ud be zurprised the volks I've done good turns by – rich and poor, old and young, all zarts comes to ol' Chellew – "

"Were you rich – once?" she interrupted him. "And then gave away all your money?"

"Rich?" he echoed in high good humour. "What, me, a land-locked ol' zeaman? No, Miss; but I helps other volks to their own riches, zee? That's my gift – and gifts be for sharing, don'ee think?" This only left her more perplexed than ever. "Now run 'ee along, Miss, there's your Nanny calling after ye."

Karla stood there with Brendy now out of his chair and pushing it headlong across flower borders, and she gave Janet a harsh talking to for speaking to strange men – "Ahrr, durrty old trremps!" – and the misdemeanour was duly reported to her mother.

"Promise me, Janet," Phillida had demanded while Brendy gloated brazenly at his sister's discomfiture, "promise me faithfully never NEVER to let yourself be spoken to by strange men in the park." Janet, while going through the motions of promising, wondered how her mother could so trustingly dispatch her to the park, full of strangers as it always was.

That the park was the haunt of shady characters she had already discovered. Once when playing hide-and-seek with Brendy she had pushed out from under some bushes in front of a bench where two men were sitting. They were trilby-hatted and their macintoshes were buttoned up although the sun shone down, and one of them held an open briefcase which was stuffed full of watches! He made a move to shut it, but seeing only a little girl – who had already seen inside, he had checked the movement and turned a smile on her that had given her a creepy feeling, while the other man had turned the case round the other way. If she had spoken to the men, she wondered, would they have stolen her, like the watches? This discovery was her secret and she had run to share it with Brendy, but the men were gone when they cautiously returned. It was just as when he had taken her to peep with secret glee at a toad sitting, with only its gullet moving, under the projecting edge of the ducks' pond, where he was not supposed to go on his own.

Then there was Karla's boyfriend who had made his appearance in the park about this time – "Pig-Face" as Brendy nicknamed him on account of the pale bristles that grew out of his nose and the pale little eyes that slid sideways at you. Pig-Face was Karla's secret from Phillida and Eric. They would sit on a bench holding hands almost silently for what seemed hours. Forgotten was Phillida's injunction to "keep an eye on the children," and they for their part would no more have told on her than they would have told on each other.

What was there to tell? – Nothing, except that Brendy had now struck up some relationship with old Chellew and seemed always bursting with some secret. "Some kind of sordid tout," was Eric's comment when, alone with her father, Janet had repeated to him Chellew's words about doing folks a good turn, which still puzzled her. What was a tout? – she wondered, but, her mother entering the room just then, she did not ask. Then there was Maizy, her very own secret: no one knew about Maizy.

On the bus to visit her granny one Saturday she had looked down into this shop window in Pennycross which was crammed with these golden-brown peasant dollies woven of broad maize leaves, and had conceived a passion to possess one of them. But her pocket money was meagre and soon spent on trifles. There was now, she found, one sure source of coins: she would hang about Karla and Pig-Face's bench until the latter would say: "Here, go and buy yourself a lolly, Janet." Then, if she dropped the coin he flipped at her with a lordly air, he would laugh at her clumsiness showing the stoppings in his teeth, and say she would never make a businesswoman. The day came when, with pockets jingling, she raced across the park, past the church and the sweet shop, turned left at the traffic light and kept on right down the road to where the shop was. She chose a little corn woman in a corn-leaf apron and holding a corn-stalk broom. Clutching her prize she raced back to the park before she was missed: Brendy, she saw, was still playing at Chellew's feet; Karla and Pig-Face were still holding hands.

With Maizy to share it, a new secret world of make-believe opened up for her. Maizy would never be seen among her other dolls, nor in the toy cupboard among Brendy's treasures. She would live in her private work-box, or under the hankies in her drawer, from which she could be smuggled into bed with her, or for a short visit, into the dolls' house.

But one day Maizy was lost. Who had discovered her? Why was she banished? Was it to punish Janet for buying her herself? They all had their secrets – Phillida had her secrets from Eric too – it wasn't fair! She would have known if Brendy had taken her from the way he looked. And Karla wouldn't dare. As for Phillida she didn't even notice Janet was sulking, though Eric shot her an enquiring glance at tea. So she was surprised when Brendy, off his own bat, said, "Why don't you ask Chellew?"

She stared at him, and he went on: "I know you've lost something because I saw you rummaging."

"That old tout? What can he do?"

"Bring things back, of course. And he's not a tout. The real touts keep away from him."

"But how can he?" she said. "I didn't even lose her in the park."

Brendy's eyes grew round with wonder. "I thought you knew," he breathed. "He brings things back for people. He calls it his gift. He got my bouncy ball for me, and Miss Lizard which that boy stole, and my crane I had for my birthday, and – lots of things."

"But how does he do it?" she kept asking.

"He sort of – whistles," was all the explanation Brendy could give.

It was raining: they could not get out on any excuse, and Chellew would not have been there. They had to wait a whole day for the chance to see him.

They found him sitting on his bench as usual.

"It's my Maizy," Janet began. "My corn dolly."

She expected him to ask questions – the sort of boring questions grown-ups always ask, but instead he stood up, suddenly very tall, towering over her.

"Just 'ee think o' your Maizy – think of her main hard – while A whistle her up."

He cupped his hands, just as she had seen him do that once, and blew – the sound was hardly a whistle; it was more like the rushing of wind, and it brought a tingling to the back of her neck which seemed to go on spreading after he had stopped. "Ah, there she is," he said at last, and sat down. "Zafe and zound as well."

"Where?"

"Look in the litter basket, dearie. Over there on the tree." Brendy started towards it, but he said: "Let your zister look, Master Brendan."

There among the wet crisp bags, lolly sticks and sweet papers, looking like a piece of discarded wrapping herself, lay Maizy. She was dry, and even slightly warm to the touch.

"But – who put her there?" Janet asked, and he laughed.

"Who put her in the basket?" he repeated. "You did, yer gummidge. Not that'n though; your mam's laundry basket. Ah, now ye remembers."

It was when she was in the bathroom and Karla came in that she had stuffed the little doll into the dirty clothes basket to hide her. Now that she had her safely back, keeping her a secret didn't seem to matter any more. And when Chellew asked her if she had lost anything else, she couldn't think of anything now that she had her Maizy. Some days later she thought of other things: a lost glove, a school library book, a talking doll she had never much cared for but wanted just for the pleasure of seeing Chellew 'whistle her up'.

But after whistling he said: "She's in good hands, Miss Janet. Another li'l gal picked her up from where 'ee left her, a poor li'l gal as ha'n't much o' her own to play with. Ye don't really want to take your ol' dolly back vrom her, do 'ee?" And it seemed just as good, knowing that this other girl had her, and sharing the secret with Chellew. This happened one evening when Eric and Phillida had gone out to a party leaving Karla to baby-sit, but she had taken the children out into the park so that she could have a secret hand-holding with Pig-Face.

"And now A must be getting off home," said Chellew.

"Where's your home?" Brendy asked. "Will you take us?"

"Ye wouldn't think it much of a home," Chellew laughed. "Down be Debnport docks. That's why A likes to come out here and zmell the zunshine."

Just then they heard a bellowing, trumpeting noise from the nearby Zoo, which was taken up by the answering howls of monkeys, or hyenas, or wolves, rising and dying away in an evening chorus.

"I wonder," began Brendy, "supposing an animal escaped from the Zoo, could you really get it back for them?"

"Don' ax me," Chellew laughed; "ax the animal." He turned to go, then hesitated. "Now run along the pair on ye, and tell Miss Karla it's your bed-time."

"Supposing it was a tiger . . ." Brendy said, as they walked back to find Karla.

NEXT morning they got up late, and while the children were having their breakfast Eric came in shouting for Phillida. Somebody had been in his workroom, he said, and taken his things. There was a great fuss and Karla was sent for and the children both had to promise they hadn't been in his workroom.

"Didn't you lock it?" asked Phillida.

"I thought I had," Eric said, "I always do."

Karla looked sheepish when she came in in her dressing gown, and it soon all came out that she had taken the children out the previous night.

"I suppose you left the front door on the latch?" said Eric.

"What's missing?" said Phillida.

"I haven't been all round yet," he said, "but the work I was on, some cufflinks and the chain I was mending for the Lord Mayor, are all gone."

"Why not ask Chellew?" Brendy piped up.

Eric stormed in his workroom: "They've been at my stones! Hell, the lapis lazuli are gone! They've even taken a small bottle of sulphuric."

"Well, the children wouldn't do that," said Phillida, "better not touch anything and send for the police."

"Why not ask Chellew?" said Brendy.

"I thought you kept all your stones locked in your safe," said Phillida.

"They've cracked it, blast them!" shouted Eric. "By God they must have had oxy-acetylene! This could only have happened when Karla took the kids out!"

Karla burst into sobs.

"Ask Chellew – Ask Chellooo," piped Brendy.

"I hope you had them all insured," said Phillida, "you know how slack you are over insurance."

"They're not insured against the house being left wide open," said Eric; "it comes to something when the child-minder walks out of the house when she's minding the children!"

"I vos tolt to mind ze chiltren, not ze jewelss!" Karla burst out.

"And leave the door on the latch?" accused Eric.

"I didn't! I didn't!" sobbed Karla.

"Would it be any good if *we* asked Chellew?" Janet asked Brendy.

"You are NOT going out by yourselves into the park!" Phillida ordered.

The police arrived. The inspector interviewed everybody separately. Karla was led sobbing forth from the ordeal. They examined Eric's workroom.

"Ask Chellew," advised Brendy. "Chellew can bring them back."

"Who's Chellew when he's at home?" a policeman asked.

"Oh, some disreputable vagrant the children seem to have taken pity on," said Phillida. "I wonder the park-keeper allows people like that to clutter up the seats."

"The park-keeper is Chellew's friend," said Brendy stoutly. "He calls him Sam."

"You could have a point there," said the inspector. "That sort of person generally keeps his eyes open. We'll have a quiet word with Mr Sam Chellew."

So a policeman opened the door and saw the children across the road. As they got to his seat they saw him just coming up the path, and before he could even sit down they were telling him about the robbery. Two policemen appeared at his side.

"Is this the man?" they asked. "We think it would be better," they said, "if the inspector conducts the enquiries. Step this way, Mr Chellew, please."

"But he can bring things back!" Brendy almost cried. "He can bring things back!"

"We'd like to think so," said the policemen; "or if he can't perhaps his friends can," and they frog-marched him towards the police car.

"Come on, Chellew, show them!" Brendy yelled through his tears. "Come on, show them you can do it!"

But the old man had changed. He panted. The colour came and went. All the old vigour and alertness and fineness of manner was drained out of the flabby old face, that fell and folded like a collapsed football. His eyes darted wildly. He babbled abjectly: " – can't help ye – can't help ye, zurr – A weren't there – A weren't there – "

"No," said the policeman," but from that bench you would be able to watch the house, wouldn't you?"

"Which houze? What houze? – Never bin near no houze – "

"The jeweller's house of course," said the inspector. "You know, the one with the brass plate – it reads: Eric Toulmin, Craftsman Jeweller."

Chellew just gibbered.

"Come along now, Mr Chellew," they said, pushing him into the police car, "you'd better come along to the station with us. You'll feel better with a nice hot cup of tea inside you."

When they had gone the house seemed stricken. Everyone got on each other's nerves. Karla shut herself up. Eric fumed. Phillida was ready to snap at everyone. Then Karla, putting a brave face on, marched the children into the park, just to be out of the way. But she made them stay by her almost as though she were afraid of finding Pig-Face there, which he wasn't. And of course there was no Chellew. Luckily Janet's school was starting again soon, and Brendy would be going with her this term.

One day in the first week of school the two of them were walking back across the park from the bus when they saw Chellew again. He stood waiting for them.

"I'm sorry – " Janet began. She felt it was all their fault that the police had taken him away. But he held up his hand.

"It don't matter now," he told her. "Not now it don't. They couldn't hold me vorever, and here A be again, like a bad penny. Just tell your dad vrom me A'm zorry A can't do nuthun about his zafe vor him. Got that? – A'm zorry A can't do nuthun about his busted zafe."

"Chellew's back!" they broke the news as they were let into the house. "We saw him just now and he said – "

But no one listened.

"A most extraordinary thing has happened," Phillida told them. "All the things that were stolen from Eric's workroom have been given back. They were just pushed through the letter box: when I came to pick up the papers, there they were, lying on the door mat!"

Who's the Ghost?

Gordon Harris-Watts

LET'S get things straight first. I'm an everyday sort of chap, I take my pleasures in moderation, I'm hale and hearty, a bachelor, and likely to remain one. I'm fifty, and strictly a loner. Mind, I believe in a chap having imagination. I like nothing better than a long walk in the country; a good pipe of St Bruno, a stout pair of boots and a stick, and I'm made.

An opportunity to do exactly this came one fine day last May. I had a day due to me from the office where I am employed by a local taxi firm. I decided to take advantage of the weather and catch one of the stopping trains to Exeter. I got to Plymouth Central, bought a ticket, visited the book stall and, armed with papers and some sandwiches from the station buffet, boarded my train. I had paid for a return to Newton Abbot, but I was putting off making the decision where to get out – this gave me a certain feeling of freedom. I sat back in my seat to glance out at the platform and the people getting on or waiting for other trains. The sun was shining, and I felt that this was going to be a real change.

As the train moved out and gradually picked up speed, the scene altered swiftly, revealing houses, and eventually fields. It was just passing through my mind that, strangely, most towns present their dirtiest face to the incoming and outgoing traveller, when the thought came to me: 'I'll get out at the first pretty stop.' I didn't have long to wait: the train slowed down and I read the halt sign: Wrangaton. 'That'll do,' I decided. I got off onto the platform, noticing that I was on my own.

As I reached the exit, there stood a railwayman. "Tickets please." He was being optimistic, mine being the only one.

"Nice day."

" 'Tis zurr, sure 'nough."

I halted by the gate. "Anything of interest around here?"

Looking at the young chap more intently, I saw he was garbed in the traditional railway uniform with the typical waistcoat with sleeves.

"Well I dunno, really." He pushed back a peaked hat, showing a mop of ginger hair. " 'Taint many gits off yurr nowadays, like it use to be. Anyways, reckon 'tis a dying spot for the likes of us yurr" – I could see that he was ready for a yarn – " 'Es, 'tis a lovely spot really though, but what with one thing and 'nother . . . you know what I mean."

I didn't, but I nodded my head in sympathy.

He went on: "Next stop's Ivybridge. You might like market day there, but yurr . . ." he seemed to look around for some echo to confirm his statement.

"You don't reckon it's worth my while looking around here then?"

He put the solitary ticket in his waistcoat pocket, took out a huge red handerchief, applied it to a well developed nose and proceeded to blow until his face took on an even ruddier hue. "Next train back'll be in three hours time, zurr; give 'ee time to stretch yer legs a bit now."

With that, he turned and shambled away to a forlorn little Victorian brick shack. I waited until he disappeared, and then walked out of the gate.

All round me was beauty. I paused for a moment, undecided as to what way to go, then finding the downhill road to be gently weaving away from the station, I took the easier choice. The hedges were high and abundant with birdlife, a sheer delight. I walked away, my pipe alight, helping to keep at bay a pet abomination of mine, the flies. The road meant an eventual destination, so I strode on, my stick swinging in harmony with my feet and a martial tune sounding in my head. This was great: the sun was shining, not a cloud was in the sky. Then, in the near distance I could distinguish the sound of a horse's hooves: clop, clop: a rhythmic addition to the harmony of nature around me. I paused in my march, and looked back as the steady clop-clop gained on me. The horse was now in sight, a fine great animal, true friend of man, and the man on his great back a typical hind, as they call them, a well set-up man with a jovial, ruddy countenance, and a straw in his mouth. As he came past me I spoke a loud "Good day to you."

At first, he seemed not to have seen me; then, he looked at me very strangely as he returned "Afternoon" in a faltering voice that was surely not the usual tone from such a lusty labourer. He said no more, but went on in an uncertain sort of way.

'He knows I'm a foreigner,' I mused; country folk are notoriously suspicious of 'emmets', as they call town folk. Still, I ought not to worry I thought, as I pressed on unabashed. I knew now that there had to be a sort of hamlet at least, somewhere ahead, for the man and his horse seemed to be on their way somewhere nearby. I strode on in their wake with the spirit of adventure on me. Then, around a bend in the road I spied just what I was looking for: a small village, perhaps not more than a hamlet, of delightful little whitewashed cottages. I slowed my pace; I certainly didn't want to march right through the place. 'Such peace!' I thought: every cottage had a thatched roof, and almost to my disbelief, there stood a pair of wooden stocks! This must belong to the National Trust, I thought. You don't often get genuine ancient monuments like this. 'What a piece of luck!' I chuckled. I looked around to ask someone the name of the place. A little boy dressed in a linen smock trotted along, driving a bevy of geese down the street. 'Queer,' I thought; 'it looks as if time has stood still here.' Then I spotted the chap who had been riding the horse, talking to a matronly woman in a poke bonnet and a white apron. He looked to me to be quite excited about something or other, judging by his gestures. Suddenly he saw me, so I started to walk over to him to inquire my whereabouts. He turned to the woman and pointed at me apparently drawing her attention to the presence of a stranger; however, she seemed to be shortsighted, and didn't seem to see me. As I approached, the man walked rapidly away. 'What strange conduct,' I thought, standing now in front of the woman.

"Good day to you," I smiled; "what a lovely little village you live in here! What do you call it?" To my surprise, she ignored me, as though I wasn't there, and walked past me into one of the cottages. 'Well I'm damned!' – I nearly exploded. I can sympathise with having little truck with strangers, but after all, I had been perfectly polite. 'There must be someone here with a bit of common manners,' I thought.

After this experience, I was now more than a bit thirsty and could have downed a pint of ale with gusto, to put my ruffled feelings to rights. So I looked round for a pub: there had to be one, I told myself; all villages have an inn. The sun was beating down strongly, and a little sit down would be welcome. A funny thing, it came to me; I hadn't noticed a bird song since coming to this place: the only birds I had seen lately were those geese the lad was herding. But what a treat, to be able to cross the street without watching out for lorries and cars! There were one or two people about now, but no one seemed interested in my presence; still I could not expect them to come rushing across the street to speak to me. Why should I complain?

No, I felt better now, and would get that pint, for just a few yards on I could see a genuine coaching inn, only needing a carriage and four outside to complete the picture-postcard eighteenth-century English pub. 'Never mind the missing coach,' I thought, as I stood for a moment outside, looking in admiration at the gabled entrance. It was covered in shingle tiles of cedar, and the oak doorframe had been carved by a master craftsman in a pattern of bunches of grapes with tendrils interwoven with vineleaves. I had never seen better carving anywhere. As I stood admiring it, two farmer types came out through the door and if I had not been quick on my feet, they would have cannoned into me. 'Manners!' I thought, as they strode out as though I wasn't there, without a word of apology, or even a glance at me. 'You can get detestable characters like that anywhere, mind.'

Striding into the bar was like going from light to dark, and I mean dark; I could barely see across the room. I tried to take in a general view of the place: the walls, roughly whitewashed, were well covered with notices of various events and advertisements of different drinks apparently on sale. I couldn't read any of them at first, as the light was so bad, although I did notice one for Waterford Porter – now that was odd – and another for Anglo-Bavarian Beer at twopence a pint. 'These must be collectors' pieces,' I thought. There were several people at the tables, all with tankards at their elbow, as you might say. Then I noticed a very fat man, pipe in one hand and tankard in the other, sitting back in an old settle. Two men were busy playing backgammon at a small table. The landlord was smoking a long clay churchwarden, and this shook me for a minute. They must have been having some sort of remembrance day or something, I thought; it was all very strange; even the young girl serving drinks, probably his daughter, had on a mob cap, as I think they used to call them.

Now I had an unpleasant feeling, just for a moment: I felt that there was something rather sinister here; not physical mind, but something. I tried to shrug off the feeling. Perhaps the landlord might be able to explain it all. 'Yet,' I demurred, 'there are no crowds, no bunting, just ordinary folk going about their leisure – it's wrong, anyhow.'

I went over to the landlord, and cheerily passed the time of day, following with my order – "A pint of your best, Landlord."

Did he answer? He bloody didn't; he carried on smoking, and then he leant over the table that served as a counter, just by me, and called across to one of the backgammon players. " 'Ave ee sin young Garge Downing s'mornin?"

"No I ain't," replied the chap at the game.

"Well," said the landlord, " 'ee reckon 'ee sin a ghost coming along to village, not half an hour ago; looked middle-age, big mind; passed 'im on farmer Steven's 'orse; 'ee reckon it passed time of day to 'im."

Several customers stopped drinking, to listen to this bit of news.

"Yes," went on the landlord, "Garge reckon he sounded funny like, dressed funny too." He stuck his pipe back in his mouth and was obviously pleased with the sensation he had caused.

Whatever stir it made on the locals, it made a far greater one on me. He had described my meeting the drover 'Garge'! What was wrong with these people? How in hell could anyone take me for a ghost? I was fifteen stone, and I stood six foot in my socks; that was enough material man for anyone, surely! No, it must have been a trick of the sunlight shining through the trees, when I met the fellow; he probably had been startled by suddenly glimpsing me with the sun in his eyes – yes, that was what had happened. I would make them laugh at the silly mistake right away.

I still stood at the table and spoke out loud and clear: "Good day to you, landlord; do I look like a ghost?" – 'Now I've shaken him,' I thought.

Well, he did take his pipe out of his mouth, but again looked right past me; in fact, I'd swear he tried to look right through me – to some old codger sipping a pint and smoking an old, dirty clay pipe. I turned to look at him, not having seen him at first. He was sitting in the dimmest corner of the bar, and creating enough smoke to warrant calling for the fire brigade. "You remember Mr Rudge, Tom, when there was talk of a ghost in the big house."

Myself, I wasn't interested in any ghost anywhere, so I said "Landlord, I've been standing here five minutes, begging you to serve me a pint of your best, and also protesting at your calling me a ghost. If you ask me, you're all acting like ghosts yourselves." Why did I say that? – But anyhow, the man didn't hear me; no man could be that rude, or deaf, and I'll swear that he didn't see me.

My mind started to turn over the events of the last half hour. It had started with the strange looks the man on the horse gave me; then, when he was talking in an agitated manner to the woman and saw me again, bolting. But nobody else seemed to see me: the two farmers had nearly collided with me, and offered no apology. This was getting a bit out of hand.

While these curious events were rushing through my mind, the old chap with the clay pipe came over to the table, and though there was plenty of room, he actually came to the spot where I was standing myself. If this had happened in a Plymouth bar, I certainly would have notified my protest in a very physical manner.

"Hey," I remonstrated, "what's the game? There's no need to shove right in front of me! Wait your turn! Let's have a bit of manners here! – What's wrong with you folk here? I'm no foreigner; I'm Devon born and bred, so how about trying to get through to this landlord of yours that I want a pint of beer, eh?"

I waited for the reaction, but there was none . . . The fool ignored me, and instead, answered the landlord's query. "Yes, I remembers that old tale; never seen it me self, mind." And there he stood, half leaning on me, almost anyhow.

I was now in a desperate mood. I cast my eyes about and spied a batch of clean pint glasses that the barmaid had just finished polishing. I strode over to grasp one. "Fill this, landlord," I shouted.

I heard a woman scream. She mouthed: "I saw it, a hand right round that there glass!" and then she fell to the floor in a faint.

Then, and only then, did I notice that my hand never actually grasped the glass; it was as though I was trying to hold a shadow; the glass was just an illusion, a ghost glass ... Or was it? The woman had screamed she saw my hand; only a hand, not me, the man. Was it because I had projected all my nervous energy entirely into the determination to get hold of the glass? No, God no, that would mean that I accepted the fact that I was a ghost - and I was not accepting that rubbish for a second! In the meantime, the landlord rushed over to where I was still standing, and then he put me in no doubt as to whether he was seeing me or not ... He put out his hand and picked up the glass that I still had my hand on; and God help me, I couldn't hold it! He had picked up what I found impossible.

The place was in chaos. The elderly woman who had fainted was on her feet again. "I swear I seed a ghostly 'and on that there glass." She was in a fair tizzy, I'll tell you.

"Steady on, me dear," soothed the landlord, " 'twas the trick of the light, I reckon."

I thought, 'The light isn't half being blamed for the damnedest things.'

A couple of burly yokels came over to where I was standing. 'Must be a favourite spot,' I thought. I've never been so crowded, in Plymouth, even on a bank holiday. Then, one of the fellows stepped on my foot, and I felt nothing! What would you think? - our feet were sharing the same space, no more - Who was the ghost? 'Hang on,' I told myself. 'I left Plymouth this morning on a day ticket; surely I would be the one to know if I were still living or not! The last lucid chat I had was with that railwayman at the station. Ever since I've been living a sort of nightmare.' Strange doubts had begun to strive to control my mind - not at first, but now, in this impossible situation that was building up in the pub. I couldn't cope much longer, I thought; things were rushing through my brain; and now I came to think about it, I realised that when I leant over to pick up that infernal glass I had no sensation of coming into contact with the wooden table any more than I had of feeling the tankard.

All this time the atmosphere in the bar was pandemonium. Several more folk had come in from the street, on hearing the rumpus, no doubt. Among them was the man they called Garge.

The landlord was onto him in a flash: "You knaw what yer said bout this ghost, Garge?"

George nodded. "Saw 'im sure nough; 'ee was walking to yure, right enough." He smiled in a sly sort of way. "Tidden many can see 'um, or talk to 'um – I kin." That sentence delivered, he looked around.

"So kin widow Awkins," spoke up another voice. "Her've sin this yur 'and over a glass, did'n her."

The old fellow with the clay pipe looked up. "I weren't lookin' or I'd 'ave seen 'en; I seed the ghost up at big house, mind 'e."

I was hemmed in all round by hulking great farm hands who were talking of no one but me, but not seeing me, and I was now in a state of panic. My forehead was damp with sweat, I felt weak at the knees, my mind was in a turmoil, and something was gravely amiss, yet I couldn't put my finger on the solution. Somehow I was certainly not welcome in this village; somehow I was different from them; and I looked around vainly for an answer. As yet, in the general uproar, the trio who claimed to be able to see ghosts had not spotted me, I noticed, but then I asked myself 'What am I saying, for Christ's sake?'

Then I spotted a clue, at last; a newspaper, that rested on a nearby table; now normally it's the current paper of the day one sees, unless it's been brought in to settle an argument. This one was in a rumpled condition, as though it had been handled by many eager readers, and now in the present panic it had become of secondary importance. In the crowd around the bar I moved, too easily I thought, to where the paper was lying. I found that my hands were not able to pick it up, sweat was now in evidence and I was in real trouble; however I could read the headlines: 'Rioting in Rochdale, Bolton, Todmorden and Stockport! Thousands of strikers burn many great mansions. The Dragoon Guards called out to suppress the mobs.' Christ! – the thing was dated August 13th, 1842. If I had found this paper under any

other conditions, I would have regarded it as a treasure, now . . .
a thousand times, no. It proved what I dreaded to know: that I
was in a world where I was alien. God only knows how this had
happened, but here were a group of simple country folk, living
quietly in their own world, and I had come among them. I was
as alive as they, so who was real, who was the ghost? Me . . . I
did not belong there, that was a fact, but I knew I was living,
thank God, and that was more than they could say . . . No, that
was not fair either: if I could only have asked each one of them,
he would have sworn he was alive . . . only, though, in this
haven of the last century.

I stood apart from the excitement, and called out as loud as I
could: "Can anyone hear me?"

Amidst the chatter and discussion, almost in unison, the old
woman, the old chap with the pipe, and my drover, my first
contact, each reacted in his or her own way: the old woman
repeated her scream, the old man dropped his pipe in his
excitement with "I yerd 'im," and the young man shouted,
"That's the man; didn'ee yurr 'im?" Now all hell was let loose;
chairs went over, glasses smashed, and good beer spilled.

Then the drover shouted, "There 'e is, over there, bold as
brass; I zee 'im!"

My mind was racing at top speed. 'What if this gets reported
in their local paper? Shall I get reported as seen in a pub, and my
grandfather not yet born? Daft, isn't it? But what do I do now?'
Perhaps the best thing would be to reason with these people –
but how I couldn't say. How about . . . 'Look here you chaps,
we have apparently got ourselves in a sticky situation,' etc. No,
the century that divided us would not allow for coherent
conversation without careful thought. I decided on a different
tack. I shouted, "My friends, please listen carefully" – I noted
that the three sensitives, as they might be called these days,
stopped their antics, and stared, fascinatedly at me, while the rest
of the folk in the bar just gaped, open mouthed, at the three.
The majority were listening to a silence, as it were, and could
only await the reactions of the three. "I am afraid that, unless I
am greatly mistaken, you will not be able to understand. I am
not a ghost, I am a living man; but you, all of you, are ghosts. I
see your newspaper is dated 13th August, 1842; I expect you call

that today's date. To me the date is 29th July, 1978. I have travelled from Plymouth today by train; I have the ticket to prove it" – and I held it up for them to see. That meant nothing to them, but the rest of my speech was told to the ones who could not see or hear. I was going to add, 'I'm sorry for you all, because you are all ghosts.' Then I realised the futility; no, to them I must be the ghost; there were too many of them; they were material to each other, and I was material only to myself with only my railway ticket to keep me sane. They would never know what I knew; I had forgotten anything they had known. It was their world, I was an alien. Give me twenty minutes out of this hole and I would be material, and they? – ghosts, forgotten, all of them. But what a pity – very pre-war beer and no way of sampling it! With that last thought, I strode boldly out through the door, leaving behind the petrified three who could see; come to think of it, why didn't I stride though the wall, to give them a last thrill? – I didn't think of that in time.

I carried on heedless, through the village, where there were still some villagers about who took no notice of me. I was a ghost, and I strode right through the village stocks, thinking it was a pity nobody could see me.

Out of the cursed place once more, I walked with a light heart towards the station, and as I went on my way my ears again were spellbound by the rich songs of the birds. I arrived at the halt and the same young porter was there; I went up to him, proffered my ticket and asked "By the way, what's the name of the village down the hill?"

"What village, zur? Bain't no village nearer than Wrangaton, and that's the other way; bain't no village that way."

I let it go.

Did I stumble through some crack in time? Certainly, the village was there, in that time, but the query will always be with me: who was the ghost?

Now dear readers, if you ever take a walk as I did, on your own, and suddenly you note that the birds have ceased their song, then you may very well find yourself in the same situation and then again the question will be:

Who's the ghost?